D0971104

AQUARIUS (Jan. 20–Feb. 18) Today your best qualities will push you into the limelight. Special meeting will bring either conflict or romance. You could find yourself under pressure. Beware!

"Come on, guys. Out with it," said Christie. "I know you aren't telling me the whole story. Why do you need *me* to run for president?"

"It's just that nobody could beat you," said Jana. "Not with your connections to Mr. Bell and your mom's being principal and all. Just think, you could go to him with a class problem, and he would listen to you."

Little explosions went off in Christie's brain, and red fireworks rained down before her eyes. It was incredible, she thought. Why did everyone expect so much of her all the time? And now . . . her own best friends . . .

"Well, ex-CUSE me," she cried, jumping to her feet. "But I just don't happen to feel like running."

For once in her life, Beth looked flustered. "It's too late," she said. "We got your nominating petitions signed when you weren't looking and turned them in this morning."

Christie was stunned. She dropped back down onto the bench like a balloon with a slow leak. My horoscope was right, she thought. I'm definitely under pressure, but it's too late to beware.

THE FABULOUS FIVE

The Popularity Trap

BETSY HAYNES

A BANTAM SKYLARK BOOK®
TORONTO · NEW YORK · LONDON · SYDNEY · AUCKLAND

RL 5, 009–012

THE POPULARITY TRAP
A Bantam Skylark Book / November 1988

*Skylark Books is a registered trademark of Bantam Books,
a division of Bantam Doubleday Dell Publishing Group, Inc.
Registered in U.S. Patent and Trademark Office and elsewhere.*

*All rights reserved.
Copyright © 1988 by Betsy Haynes and James Haynes.
Cover art copyright © 1988 by Ralph Amatrudi.
No part of this book may be reproduced or transmitted
in any form or by any means, electronic or mechanical,
including photocopying, recording, or by any information
storage and retrieval system, without permission in
writing from the publisher.
For information address: Bantam Books.*

ISBN 0-553-15634-9

Published simultaneously in the United States and Canada

*Bantam Books are published by Bantam Books, a division of Bantam Doubleday Dell
Publishing Group, Inc. Its trademark, consisting of the words "Bantam Books" and the
portrayal of a rooster, is Registered in U.S. Patent and Trademark Office and in other
countries. Marca Registrada. Bantam Books, 666 Fifth Avenue, New York, New York 10103.*

PRINTED IN THE UNITED STATES OF AMERICA

S   0 9 8 7 6 5 4 3 2 1

The Popularity Trap

CHAPTER

1

"Oh, no," moaned Christie Winchell. "Here comes Mr. Bell. I'll absolutely die if he speaks to me in front of everybody again." She looked around the corridor of Wakeman Junior High for some way to be inconspicuous. A drinking fountain where her face would be hidden. An empty classroom to duck into. Anything, just so he wouldn't notice her, but of course, she was out of luck.

"I don't know why you're so paranoid over the principal's speaking to you," muttered her friend Katie Shannon. "I'd be thrilled if he spoke to me, much less smiled and called me by name."

Christie groaned. She started to explain to Katie how embarrassing it was to be singled out by the principal just because your mother was also a school principal, and because he knew Mrs. Winchell personally. But by now Mr. Bell was within earshot and smiling broadly at her.

"Hi there, Christie," he called out, causing a few students in the hallway to glance at her and smirk. "How are you today?"

"Fine, thank you, Mr. Bell," she mumbled.

"Well, that's great," he boomed. "Just *great*."

"That's great. Just *great*," mimicked Clarence Marshall as he zoomed around the girls on his way to the cafeteria. Calling back over his shoulder, he added, "Must be nice to be the principal's pet!"

"See what I mean?" snapped Christie. It had been tough enough being the principal's daughter during the years she was at Mark Twain Elementary, but at least her mother had never embarrassed her by singling her out in front of the rest of the school. Why couldn't Mr. Bell figure out a thing like that? Still, when she had complained about it at home, her parents had assured her that it was both an honor and a responsibility to be a school principal's child. An honor and a responsibility? she had thought later. Baloney. What it *was* was a pain!

The lunchroom was crowded as Christie and Katie pushed their way in. Seventh-grade lunch period was always a zoo, but luckily Christie quickly spotted the rest of their friends at a table near the back. The Fabulous Five, as their clique was called, had been best friends almost forever. Besides Christie and Katie, the group consisted of Jana Morgan, Beth Barry, and Melanie Edwards. Christie had to smile every time she thought about how different they were from each other. She knew that she was considered quiet and brainy, just the opposite of boisterous, theatrical Beth. Melanie was more interested in boys than anything else on earth, which really bugged Katie, the feminist of the group. And Jana was the peacemaker, the leader in many ways.

"Guess what, Christie?" called Beth as Christie and Katie reached the lunch table. Beth's eyes were huge, and she looked as if she were about to burst with excitement. "We're nominating you to run for class president! Isn't that great?"

"Terrific," said Katie, giving Christie a hearty slap on the back. "Christie Winchell for seventh-grade president of Wacko Junior High. It has a nice ring to it."

"Whoa!" said Christie, doing a double take. "What are you talking about? I don't want to be president of the seventh-grade class."

"We have it all figured out," Beth went on, completely ignoring Christie's objections. "We'll run your campaign. We've already started working on slogans."

"Right," Melanie chimed in. "What do you think of, 'You can't miss if you vote for Chris'?"

"I'm not Chris. I'm Christie," she insisted. "And besides, you weren't listening. I *said*—I don't want to run for class president."

"Wait until you hear who else is running," said Jana. "Mandy McDermott from Copper Beach Elementary is running for vice president, Elizabeth Harvey from Riverfield is running for secretary, and Richie Corrierro is running for treasurer. They're all okay, especially Richie since he's from Mark Twain, but Melissa McConnell, the most perfect member of the human race, is running for president. There's no way we can let her win."

Christie plunked her lunch bag onto the table and sank on the bench with a sigh. Was this what her horoscope had meant? she wondered. She had read it so eagerly this morning before leaving for school and had felt so tingly over the romance part that she had memorized every word.

> *Aquarius (Jan. 20–Feb. 18): Today your best qualities will push you into the limelight. Special meeting will bring either conflict or romance. You could find yourself under pressure. Beware!*

Still, her friends had been right about one thing. Melissa McConnell would make a terrible president. She had the reputation of being a total perfectionist, all right. Not only was she a straight A student, but everything about her was perfect. Her hair was always perfectly styled. Her clothes were always perfectly matched. Even her handwriting was perfectly legible. It was disgusting. What's more, she would probably expect everyone in the class to be as perfect as she was if she was elected president.

But the worst thing about Melissa was the fact that she was one of The Fantastic Foursome, another clique of seventh-grade girls who had set themselves up as major rivals of The Fabulous Five on the very first day of school. Their leader was Laura McCall, who was tall and pretty and wore her blond hair in one long braid that started on top of her head and fell practically to her waist. Everyone said that Laura made the other three girls, Tammy Lucero, Funny Hawthorne, and Melissa, do certain things to stay in her clique, but no one knew exactly what those things were.

"I hear what you're saying," said Christie. Then she opened her arms and raised her shoulders in a giant shrug. "But why me?"

"You're a natural," offered Melanie.

"You're smart and well organized," said Beth. "And believe me, being well organized is essential."

Christie shook her head. "You guys are putting me on. I'm not the one who should be running. Jana, you're a good leader. Why don't we nominate you?"

"Thanks, Christie, but I'm seventh-grade coeditor of the yearbook, remember?"

"So?" said Christie.

"So—I'm going to be awfully busy," Jana insisted. "Working on *The Wigwam* is a big job, and I want to do it right."

Katie's eyes brightened. "Just think, if both the class president and the seventh-grade coeditor of the yearbook are from The Fabulous Five, we'll show The Fantastic Foursome a thing or two."

"And don't forget that Beth and I are cheerleaders," Melanie said proudly.

"Okay, then why not nominate Katie?" suggested Christie. "Class president is her kind of job."

"Actually, I thought about running," Katie admitted. "But I hear that Mr. Bell is thinking about forming a Teen Court to deal with kids who get in trouble at school. Three students from each class will be on it, along with some teachers. I'd rather try for that."

"It figures," muttered Christie. "But I still don't see why *I* have to run for president. There are lots of kids who would make better presidents than Melissa McConnell. How about some of the boys? Randy Kirwan, for instance? Or Scott Daly? Or Shane Arrington? I'd vote for any of them."

"Randy would make a great president," said Jana. "And I'm not saying that just because he's my boyfriend, either. But don't forget, he plays sports all year long. He wouldn't have time to be president."

Melanie had rolled her eyes when she heard Christie mention two of the boys she had crushes on. "The same goes for Shane and Scott," she added in a dreamy voice. "But wouldn't it be fun to be the class president's girlfriend?" She paused and gazed toward the ceiling. "Would that make me 'the First Girlfriend'?"

"So we're back to you, Christie," said Beth, ignoring Melanie's question. "You have to do it. Besides, we really need you."

"Come on, guys. Out with it," said Christie. "I know you aren't telling me the whole story. Why do you need *me*?"

Beth lowered her eyes. Melanie squirmed and shuffled her feet, and all four of them looked suddenly uncomfortable.

When no one answered, Christie took a deep breath and put her hands on her hips. "I asked you a question. Why do you need me?" she repeated.

"It's just that nobody could beat you," said Jana. "Not with your connections to Mr. Bell. Just think, you could go to him with a class problem, and he would listen to you."

Little explosions went off in Christie's brain, and red fireworks rained down before her eyes. It was incredible, she thought. Why did everyone expect so much of her all the time? And now . . . her own best friends . . .

"Well ex-CUSE me," she cried, jumping to her feet. "But I just don't happen to feel like running."

For once in her life Beth looked flustered. "It's too late," she said. "We got your nominating petitions signed when you weren't looking and turned them in this morning."

Christie was stunned. She dropped back down onto the bench like a balloon with a slow leak. My horoscope was right, she thought. I'm definitely under pressure, but it's too late to beware.

CHAPTER

2

*C*hristie had never felt so alone in her life as she nibbled on her tuna sandwich and listened to her friends making campaign plans. Their excited chatter swirled around her as if she weren't even sitting with them.

"We've got to make signs and come up with a slogan," said Beth. "Now everybody *think*."

"What we need is a gimmick," said Katie. "You know, a way to tie Christie's name in with something everybody knows."

"If she spelled Christie with a *K* instead of a *C*, we could call her Special K," offered Melanie. "You know, 'Vote for Special K.' We could even cut the words off cereal boxes and wear them as campaign buttons."

9

"But her name is Christie with a *C*," Jana reminded them.

"I've got it!" shouted Melanie, banging her fist on the table so hard that her milk carton jumped. "C! Vitamin C! How about 'Cure all your troubles with Vitamin C'?"

Christie glanced up, making a face, and Katie nodded in agreement. Pure cornball, thought Christie. Absolutely the pits.

"Does anybody have a better idea?" Melanie asked defensively. When nobody said anything, she went right on talking. "We could make all the posters round and orange to go with the idea of vitamin C." She looked around proudly to see if everyone was getting her message.

A light came on in Beth's eyes. "In *fact*, we could even give away oranges!" she shouted. Then she lowered her voice, as if she was worried that another candidate would overhear and steal the idea. "That's it, guys. Lots of kids give away things when they run for office. We could write Christie's name on little stickers and put them on the oranges. Then we could give one to every seventh-grader."

"A day without Christie is like a day without sunshine," Jana sang, and Christie knew that no matter how she felt about being known as Vitamin C, her fate was sealed.

Sighing, she absently broke her sandwich into a

dozen pieces while she thought about her situation. First, she did not want to run for class president, but her friends were railroading her into it. Second, building her campaign around vitamin C hinted that she would be some kind of cure-all who could fix things with Mr. Bell because he knew her personally. Nothing could be further from the truth. She couldn't fix things if she wanted to, and what's more, she wouldn't—even if she could.

"I still wish you would nominate someone else," she said. "It really bugs me that you guys sneaked around getting petitions signed without even asking me."

"Sorry, but we explained," said Melanie. "We've already turned in your petitions to the office. There's nothing we could do about it now, even if we wanted to."

"Maybe we could talk to Mr. Bell . . ." Christie began, but stopped herself as she saw slow smiles spreading across her friends' faces.

"See," said Beth. "What did we tell you? Listen, Christie. Nominating you for class president is the greatest idea we've ever had."

"Don't you get it?" Jana asked. "Anytime something goes wrong, all you have to do is talk to your *friend*, Mr. Bell. There's no way Melissa McConnell can compete with something like that."

Christie felt her anger rising to the boiling point. "Well, she can have it. Maybe I won't even try to win."

But the instant the words were out, she felt a stab of guilt. Her four friends had turned to each other with looks of dismay. I can't throw the election, she thought, and let my best friends down. Out loud she murmured, "I'll try to win. I promise I will. I know how much it means to you guys."

"Terrific," said Katie.

"We knew you'd go along with it once you thought it over," Melanie assured her.

While the others went back to their campaign planning, Christie poked at the pieces of her tuna sandwich, pushing them back together like pieces of a jigsaw puzzle. She stirred uneasily, suddenly feeling as if someone across the lunchroom was staring at her.

Glancing up, she half expected it to be Melissa McConnell looking over the competition. But to her total surprise the eyes she met were not Melissa's. They didn't even belong to another girl. The person looking at her so intently was Jon Smith, the boy she had been noticing ever since the beginning of school, and whom she had caught looking at her three whole times last Saturday night at Laura McCall's party.

Jon was one of the quietest boys in seventh grade, which seemed strange to most kids since his parents were both local television personalities and anything but quiet themselves. His father, Chip Smith, was sports director and interviewed famous athletes all the time. His mother, who went by the name Marge Whitworth, was a news anchorwoman and had her own late-afternoon talk show. Christie couldn't help but be a little bit impressed. Besides, she argued to herself, he was awfully cute, and being quiet was no big deal. She was quiet herself.

Instantly she felt a little foolish as they continued to look straight at each other. How should she react? Should she smile at him? Maybe even try to flirt? But he wasn't smiling at her. In fact, he looked as if he was angry. His face looked stiff and his jaws were clenched.

That's ridiculous, she thought, looking away. I've never done anything to him. We've never even spoken to each other. Then she smiled as another thought occurred to her. Did Jon Smith want to run for class president? And did he know he didn't have a chance because she had connections with Mr. Bell?

The idea made her blush. Don't be silly! she told herself silently. I *don't* have connections to Mr. Bell. And even if I did, maybe Jon would win, anyway. I'll bet lots of kids would vote for him if they thought he would introduce them to his parents or let them hang around and meet famous people.

Just then the loudspeaker at the other end of the cafeteria crackled to life. "Attention, please. Attention, please," said Miss Simone, the school secretary. "Will Christie Winchell please report to Mr. Bell's office?"

Christie rose slowly, avoiding the I-told-you-so looks that she knew would be on her friends' faces. This is all I need, she thought angrily. Now everyone will be more convinced than ever that I have an "in" with the principal. She couldn't help glancing toward the spot where Jon Smith had been sitting a moment ago to see if he was looking at her that way, too, but to her surprise he was gone.

CHAPTER

3

"What's that all about?" asked Jana.

Christie shrugged. "You've got me."

"Maybe he's going to ask your opinion about something," Melanie said with a giggle. "You know. Which teachers to fire. Or how many extra days of vacation we should have this year."

"How many extra days of vacation we *deserve*, you mean," said Beth. Then seeing that Christie had gathered up her lunch trash and was about to leave the table, she added, "Go get 'em, Vitamin C!"

Christie made her way through the crowded cafeteria, hoping that no one had heard Beth call her Vitamin C. She still might be able to convince them to take her name off the list of candidates. In fact, she might even talk to Mr. Bell herself and ask him what she could do to withdraw. Christie cringed. That would be using her relationship with the principal exactly the way her friends said she could. Which was worse? she wondered. Using it for personal problems or using it to help the entire seventh-grade class?

"Hi, Christie," called Alexis Duvall from a table near the door. "I hear you're running for class president."

Christie stopped beside Alexis's table. It was crowded with kids she knew—Kim Baxter, Lisa Snow, Sara Sawyer, Gloria Drexler, and Marcie Bee. They were all looking at her and smiling.

Nodding, she said, "My friends in The Fabulous Five nominated me. I didn't even know they were doing it."

"Yeah, we know," said Marcie. "We signed your petitions. We knew your friends were doing it in secret, but we didn't know if they had told you yet. I think it's super that they did a thing like that for you. It proves how much they like you if they even want you to be president."

"I'll vote for you," volunteered Sara. "Especially since you're running against *Melissa McConnell*." She held her nose and made a face as if she were smelling something putrid, and all around the table girls began holding their noses and nodding their heads in agreement.

"We'll all vote for you for president and Richie Corrierro for treasurer," said Alexis. "And if you need help with posters or anything, just let us know."

The others were nodding and smiling again. It made Christie feel surprisingly good.

"Thanks, guys. I have to get going now," she said, moving toward the door. It was nice to know that so many kids were planning to vote for her. Maybe running for class president wouldn't be so bad after all, she thought.

She had almost reached the swinging doors leading into the hallway when someone stepped in front of her. It was Laura McCall, and following her like a parade of ducks were the rest of The Fantastic Foursome.

"Hello, Christie," Laura said crisply.

"Hi," she responded.

"We hear that you're running against Melissa for class president."

"So . . . ?" said Christie.

"So—don't get any big ideas about winning," said Laura. "We're planning such a terrific campaign for her that you couldn't beat her in a million years."

"That's right." Melissa snickered. "Just wait until you hear my slogan. 'Vote for Melissa McConnell for president when you care enough to elect the very best.'" Her nose was in the air and she was giving Christie a superior look.

Christie didn't answer. She looked straight at Melissa and thought, It fits. Voting for her is like sending an April Fools' Day card.

"So what's your slogan?" Laura challenged.

Christie pulled herself up to her full height and tried to act proud. "My slogan is 'Cure all your troubles with Vitamin C.' C stands for Christie, of course."

The Fantastic Foursome just stared at her for a moment. Then Laura burst out laughing, and the others did, too.

"Vitamin C!" shrieked Tammy Lucero. "What are you, a piece of fruit?"

"Sure," said Melissa. "She's gone bananas. Everybody knows that."

Christie could feel her face turning a bright shade of red. It had been one thing to make a joke out of Melissa's slogan, but hearing her own turned around into something stupid really burned her up. "Just wait," she said, stomping past them. "I'll beat the socks off of you."

She was still smarting from the encounter with The Fantastic Foursome when she got to the principal's office. Barreling in without looking right or left, she went straight to the reception desk and started to tell Miss Simone who she was.

"Don't bother sitting down, Christie," said the secretary before Christie could say her name. "Mr. Bell is waiting for you."

"Great," Christie grumbled to herself. "I even get the red-carpet treatment from the principal's secretary."

Mr. Bell stood up and smiled cordially when Christie entered his office. He was tall and slim with a patch of shiny scalp poking up through close-cropped gray hair.

"Hello there, Christie," he said. "Have a seat and tell me how your parents are getting along."

"Just fine, thank you," said Christie. Talking so informally with the principal made her feel self-conscious.

Mr. Bell leaned toward her and lowered his voice to confidential tones. "I have a special favor to ask you," he said, and Christie heard warning sirens going off in her brain. What next? she wanted to shout.

"You are a superior math student," the principal went on, "and I have been approached by the parents of one of our young men. Frankly, they feel their son needs help. He's a seventh-grader like yourself, and he's having a little trouble catching on to the math principles you're studying right now. I would consider it a personal favor if you would agree to tutor him a couple of days a week after school."

Christie wasn't sure if she groaned out loud or only in her mind. How could he ask her to do a thing like that? Tutoring little kids was one thing, but a boy in her own class? It would be totally embarrassing for both of them.

"I doubt if you know him," said Mr. Bell, as if he had read her mind. "He went to Copper Beach Elementary."

"But Mr. Bell . . ." Christie started to protest.

"I assured the parents that you were the sort of person who would be only too happy to help their son. And of course, as I said before, I would consider it a personal favor."

Trapped! thought Christie. Trapped for the second time today. First she had been trapped into running for class president, and now she was trapped into tutoring some jerk!

"I hope it won't take up much time," she said. "I'm running for president of the seventh-grade class, and I don't have a lot of spare time. In fact, maybe you should look for someone who isn't so busy."

Mr. Bell beamed at her. "Class president, eh? That's wonderful. And it also proves that you're exactly the sort of person this young man's parents are looking for. I'm sure you'll be a great influence on him."

The principal didn't notice Christie roll her eyes as he went to the door and motioned for someone to come into his office. It's probably the kid himself, she thought angrily. The "young man," as Mr. Bell had called him. The jerk!

"Christie Winchell," said Mr. Bell, "I'd like for you to meet Jon Smith."

Christie was stunned. She lowered her gaze from the ceiling very slowly and looked into the same face that had stared at her in the cafeteria. Jon Smith was still scowling, and now she knew why.

CHAPTER

4

"I know you two are going to hit it off just fine," said Mr. Bell, smiling and rising from his chair.

Christie felt her heart begin to pound. Jon Smith's sullen expression hadn't changed. If this was the meeting her horoscope had mentioned—the part about a special meeting that would bring either conflict or romance—she had the definite feeling that it was going to be conflict instead of romance.

"If you'll excuse me, I have some business in another part of the school," the principal went on. "Feel free to use my office for the rest of lunch period to get acquainted and set up a schedule for getting together."

"I'm busy after school today," Christie said hurriedly when Mr. Bell had left the room. Actually that wasn't true. It was just that she needed more time. All she could think about now was how embarrassed she was over the whole thing.

"I'm busy, too," mumbled Jon, frowning.

Christie started to say that she couldn't do it tomorrow, either, but she stopped herself. After all, she reasoned, she couldn't put it off forever. She had to do it sometime. She might as well get it over with.

"Tomorrow is okay for me," she offered.

Jon looked down at the floor for a moment, and Christie suspected that he was thinking about putting it off, too. "Okay," he said reluctantly. "Where do you want to meet?"

Christie bit her lower lip and thought for a moment. "Um . . . how about a back booth at Bumpers?"

"NO!"

Eeek! she thought. Bad move. He doesn't even want to be seen with me. She tried not to let him see how flustered she was, locking her hands into tight fists and hiding them behind her back. "Well, you can come to my house if you want to. Nobody will see us there."

Jon shrugged. "Sure," he said. "Where do you live?"

Christie gave him the address, which he wrote on a small scrap of paper and stuck into his shirt pocket. Turning to leave, he paused when he reached the door and said, "Don't think this was my idea, because it wasn't." Without waiting for her to respond, he was gone.

"It wasn't my idea, either!" she called, knowing that he was probably too far down the hall to hear her. The nerve! she thought. I shouldn't have to apologize for something I was pressured into doing.

After school Christie met Katie and Jana, and together they walked to Bumpers for a soda. Bumpers was the fast food restaurant where the kids from junior high hung out. It had gotten its name from the brightly painted bumper cars, relics of an old amusement park ride, that were hanging from the ceiling and spaced around the floor for kids to sit in. Christie sat in a green one with Jana, while Katie sat in the booth they wanted to hold until Beth and Melanie arrived from cheerleading practice.

After they had ordered cherry colas Christie gave Katie and Jana a helpless look. "How do I get myself into these things?" she wailed. "I don't want to tutor Jon Smith."

Katie frowned. "It's your fault for letting Mr. Bell pressure you into it. You should have explained to him how you feel. He would have listened to you."

"Huh," scoffed Christie. "Fat chance."

"Don't forget that you've been dying to meet Jon," said Jana. "It's the perfect opportunity for you to make an impression on him."

Christie started to protest, but Jana wasn't finished yet. "Don't kid us," she said with a knowing grin. "You have a crush on him and you know it."

Someone punched a number on the old Wurlitzer jukebox, and rock music blasted out, making conversation impossible. Christie was glad. She didn't really want to talk about Jon. It was true that she had noticed him, just the way Jana had said, and she did think he was awfully cute. But his rotten attitude toward her tutoring him had given her second thoughts. Besides, their tutoring sessions could make any chance of a relationship between them impossible.

Kids were still pouring into Bumpers, and a few minutes later Melanie and Beth scooted into the booth and sat across from Katie.

"Gosh. Cheering is so much fun," gushed Melanie. She was breathless, and her cheeks were still pink from all the exercise. "I can't wait until the first game. I'll be *so* excited that I'll die."

"Greetings, girls," said a familiar voice from over Christie's left shoulder.

She didn't have to look around to know who it was. Only nerd-of-the-world Curtis Trowbridge would say "greetings" when a simple "hi" would do.

"Hi, Curtis," said Beth. "What's up?"

"Actually it's Christie I want to talk to," said Curtis with a wink. "But the rest of you can listen in."

Curtis whipped a small notebook out of his back pocket and a pencil from behind one ear and looked at

Christie thoughtfully. "I'm on the school newspaper staff, you know, and I've been assigned to do a story for *The Wakeman Smoke Signal* on the candidates for president of our class," he said importantly. "And I'd like to interview you about your campaign platform."

Christie was astonished. "You *what?*" she gasped. "Curtis, I just found out today that I've been nominated. I don't have any campaign platform. I don't even want the job."

"Don't print that!" Katie commanded, putting her hand out in a halting gesture. She slid out of the booth and stationed herself with folded arms between Curtis and Christie, looking as if she would grab the pencil out of Curtis's hand if he wrote down what Christie had just said.

"Of course she has a platform," Katie went on. "It's a great platform. She just hasn't worked out all the details yet. We don't want to start talking about it too soon, so how about giving us a little more time?"

Curtis shrugged. "Sure," he said. "I'll interview Melissa now and get back to you on Wednesday at school."

After Curtis left, Christie gave Katie a puzzled look. "What were you talking about?" she demanded. "I don't have any platform."

"So? It made Curtis happy, didn't it? We'll think up one," said Beth. "Come on over to the booth, and we can talk about it."

"I see this as a perfect opportunity for you to stand up for the rights of girls," said Katie once Jana and Christie had settled into the booth.

Melanie wrinkled her nose. "Katie Shannon," she scolded. "You can be so boring sometimes. Nobody wants to hear all that junk. Besides, if she did what you say, probably none of the boys would vote for her. And don't forget, they're half the class."

"What we need to do is come up with something dramatic," said Beth, opening her eyes wide with excitement. "You know, something that will really get everybody's attention."

"Do you mean something like eliminating physical education from the curriculum?" Jana teased. "Or making lunch period two hours long?"

"You've got it!" Beth said, laughing. "Only it has to be something that kids want and that Christie can deliver."

"Well, I can't deliver Mr. Bell, if that's what you're getting at. If I could, I wouldn't be in this mess with Jon Smith." Christie sighed. She had had enough talk about Jon Smith and her running for class president, and she certainly didn't like the suggestions her friends wanted to put into her platform much less into an article for the *Sig*, as most kids called the *Wakeman Smoke Signal*. "I'll see you guys later," she said, getting up to leave. "I'm going home to do my homework. And do you know what? For the first time in my life, I'm actually looking forward to it."

Everyone called good-bye as Christie headed for the door, waving to a few other friends on her way. She was so preoccupied with her own problems that she almost bumped into someone coming into Bumpers as she was going out the door. Looking up, she saw to her astonishment that it was Jon Smith.

He scowled and brushed on past her. Christie clutched her books and felt her face turning red. Here she was at Bumpers after she had told him that she was too busy to tutor him after school today. *But*, she reflected, that was what he had told her, too.

CHAPTER

5

When she got home, Christie dumped her books on her desk and flopped down on her bed. What a pain. She really *needed* to be campaigning for seventh-grade president of Wacko Junior High along with trying to keep all A's in school, she thought sarcastically. What would everyone think if she stopped doing her homework and dropped out of the elections? It would be great not to have to worry about what other people wanted and concentrate on what she liked to do for a change. But that would mean disappointing her friends and her mom and dad.

At first she had missed Mark Twain Elementary where everything had been so comfortable and familiar, but lately she had been starting to enjoy junior high school. It had seemed so much more grown-up than elementary school. And she had begun to believe that she would have more freedom now. What a joke! Getting up, she went to her desk and resolutely opened her math book.

"Hi, sweetheart. I'm home." Mrs. Winchell stuck her head in the doorway of Christie's room.

"Hi, Mom."

"Doing your homework, I see." Her mother made that comment at this time just about every day. "How was your day?"

"Fine." Christie smiled at her mother. She was a super mom. It was just that she was always checking to see if Christie was keeping up with everything.

"I saw Mr. Bell today. He said you volunteered to tutor another student in math. That's really nice of you, dear. Not all gifted people take time to help others. I'm proud of you. Oh, and he also told me that you were running for class president. That's great. Why didn't you tell us you were going to run?"

Christie smiled again, weakly. "I didn't know it myself." She decided against telling her mother that she hadn't volunteered for either job. After all, hadn't her mother just gotten through saying how proud she was of Christie? There was no use bursting her bubble.

Later, at the dinner table, her father asked, "What do you say to some tennis on Saturday, Christie? George Ellis and I were talking at the office. He was captain of the Dartmouth tennis team, and when I asked him if he'd help you with your backhand, he said he'd be delighted. Maybe we can get in a few sets afterwards. You know, to tune up your game a little."

"Vince, Christie may have to study on Saturday," said Mrs. Winchell. "She has volunteered to tutor another student, and I might add, our daughter is running for class president."

"Great!" Her father looked at Christie with pleasure. "I was president of one of my classes. Hmmm. I can't remember which one it was now, though."

"Well," her mother continued, "we just have to make sure she has time to keep up her grades. She's doing better than either Michael or Edward when they were her age, and we don't want to overburden her so she can't keep it up."

Christie cringed. Her mother was always comparing her with her two older brothers, one of whom was in medical school and the other was a lawyer. She was glad that her parents had faith in her abilities, but keeping up with Mike and Ed was a real burden sometimes.

Christie finally finished her homework and closed her books at ten o'clock. She had done all of her assignments, and since Jon Smith might be as much as two chapters behind in math, she reviewed chapters five and six so she would be ready to help him.

She climbed into bed, thinking about all that was happening to her. She loved most of the things she was doing. School was fun. She had the best friends in the world in Jana, Melanie, Katie, and Beth. The Fabulous Five had been together since they were in the lower grades at Mark Twain. They had all been so excited about going into junior high. They just knew that if they stuck together, it would be more fun than Mark Twain Elementary.

But then they ran into Laura McCall and The Fantastic Foursome on the very first day of school. The two cliques had been enemies ever since. When The Fantastic Foursome put Melissa McConnell up for class president, The Fabulous Five just had to put someone up, too. Otherwise they would be run over. But why did Christie have to be the one? She had as much to do as the others. Maybe more with her mom and dad's pushing her. Junior high was a lot more complicated than elementary school.

Playing tennis was fun, too, or it could be. She loved playing it with her father. It was just that he kept bringing in other people to teach her things and talking about how young some of the great tennis pros were, as if he expected her to start competing any day now. That ruined it for her. She hated to tell him she just wanted to play and have fun. She knew it would hurt his feelings.

She just hoped that her mother wouldn't spread the word among her friends that Christie was tutoring someone and running for class president. Jon was unhappy with her already. If he thought she was spreading the word that he was dumb, he'd hate her. If everyone would *just leave her alone*.

She pulled the covers up under her chin and concentrated on going to sleep.

Beth and Katie came running up to Christie as soon as she stepped onto the school ground the next morning.

"Christie! Guess what Laura McCall and her friends have done! You won't believe it!" cried Beth. "They've put stickers that say Melissa McConnell for president on all the seventh-grade lockers!"

Jana and Melanie joined them just as Katie was saying, "Yeah, and that includes our lockers, too. It was probably that witch Laura McCall's idea."

"What includes our lockers, too?" asked Jana. Beth retold her story with all the drama she could muster.

"What are we going to do?" asked Melanie.

"Not get overly excited, for one thing," said Jana, looking at Beth. "The first thing we've got to take care of is those stickers, and then we've got to have a meeting of The Fabulous Five and plan Christie's campaign strategy. We can meet at my apartment after school. Has anybody got any ideas about what to do about the stickers?"

"I do," said Christie. She might as well join in the planning if she was going to have to run, she thought. "Melanie, do you still have all those big happy-face stickers you got for your birthday?" asked Christie.

"Yes. They're in my locker."

"Why don't we write on them and stick them on over Melissa's stickers?"

"Great idea," said Jana. "If we hurry, we can get it done before homeroom."

"What will we write on them?" asked Katie.

"I know," said Melanie. "'Vote for Christie—She's Got the Connections.'"

Christie's stomach turned over. She had to get them off that kick before everyone in the whole school was calling her the principal's pet.

Christie met her friends at their usual table in the cafeteria. They had divided up the happy-face stickers and had each taken a section of hallway where the seventh-grade lockers stood. Then they had scurried around, slapping stickers on lockers, being sure to cover up Melissa McConnell's stickers, all the way to the lunchroom.

"We did it!" shouted Beth when all five of them had reached the table.

"The Fantastic Foursome are just simply going to die when they see our stickers," Jana said with a confident laugh.

Melanie giggled. "I put two on Shane Arrington's locker and I even put one on Garrett Boldt's locker, even though he's an eighth-grader and can't vote for Christie."

"What a waste!" said Katie, glaring at Melanie.

Christie listened to her friends' happy chatter, but she didn't feel like joining in. She only ate half of her tuna sandwich and stuffed the other half back into her lunch bag to put into the garbage. Her appetite was gone. Now that those stickers were on the lockers, there would be no way to back out of the election. She was definitely trapped this time, and what made it even worse, she had helped.

"Let's chip in our change and stop and get some more stickers on the way to Jana's apartment," Beth was saying as Christie tuned in again.

"Good idea," said Jana. "I've got markers and we can work at the kitchen table."

"Can I bring my new album?" asked Beth. "We can put it on the stereo in your room and turn it up so we can hear it in the kitchen."

"Sure," said Jana. "But what's Laura doing?"

Christie looked toward the table where The Fantastic Foursome were sitting. Laura McCall was half standing, with one knee on the bench, and she was talking excitedly to Melissa, Funny, and Tammy.

"She probably just found out about our stickers on top of theirs," said Katie, laughing. "Boy, I'll bet she's mad."

Laura glanced at The Fabulous Five and smirked. She was flicking her long, blond braid back and forth the way a cat flicked the end of its tail while it stalked its prey. Christie had a creepy feeling that what Laura had been talking to her friends about wasn't stickers.

CHAPTER

6

*A*s Christie watched, Laura McCall turned to Funny, Melissa, and Tammy and nodded. Tammy picked up a large brown paper bag that had been sitting on the floor, and each of the girls dipped into it and pulled out ribbons in bright shades of pink and yellow and green. Then they started handing them out to all the seventh-graders in the cafeteria.

"What are they doing?" cried Beth as Laura worked her way toward their table.

"Whatever it is, I don't like it," said Jana. "She's putting one on Randy!" Laura was bending over Randy Kirwan and pinning a ribbon to his sweater, and he was smiling at her.

36

When Laura got to their table, she said with a sneer, "I'm sure you'll want these, too." She tossed several brightly colored ribbons into the middle of the table and with a flip of her long braid, went on to the next table.

Christie looked at the ribbons as if they were poison.

"What do they say?" asked Melanie.

"What do you expect them to say?" Christie answered, picking up one. "They're campaign ribbons." She read the card, decorated with a hand-colored rainbow, that was pinned to the top of the ribbon in her hand:

"'Vote for Melissa McConnell for Seventh-Grade Class President, If You Care Enough to Elect the Very Best.'"

"The very *worst*, you mean!" said Katie, ripping the card off the ribbon and stuffing both inside her empty chocolate milk carton.

"She pinned that ribbon on Randy just to make me mad," said Jana, her voice rising.

"Don't get on her case for being ahead of us," Christie answered, even though she was getting angry, too. She didn't like anyone's humiliating her and her friends, and that's just what The Fantastic Foursome were doing.

"It's time for us to get our act together. If I'm going to run, let's do it right. Everyone can be at Jana's after school, right?"

Her four friends nodded.

"I'll talk to Lisa Snow and Kim Baxter and see if they can come," offered Katie. "They signed the nominating petitions, and I know they'd like to help."

"I'll talk to Sara Sawyer in my gym class," said Melanie. "Jana, don't you have classes with Alexis Duvall and Mona Vaughn?"

"Right," said Jana. "Leave them to me."

"I'll talk to Jon and see if he can come after supper," Christie said. She hated to put him off again, but planning her campaign was getting serious.

Christie saw looks of determination on her friends' faces. Look out, Laura McCall and friends! she thought.

Jana's mother wouldn't be home from work for an hour or so, so The Fabulous Five and their friends had the apartment to themselves. Jana got sodas out of the refrigerator and went to get her markers. Beth and Melanie picked out records and turned the stereo up high while Christie and Katie organized the things they had bought on the way from school on the kitchen table. Jon had only grunted when Christie asked him if he could come over after dinner instead of right after school. She guessed he had meant yes.

"I get to work on the happy-face stickers," sang Beth.

"Me, too!" echoed Sara and Alexis.

"Why don't we all do it," said Jana. "Then we can work on the posters together, too."

"I see you did get orange poster board," said Christie.

"Sure. We'll cut them into circles and put faces on them so they'll look like oranges, and we'll write the slogans at the top and bottom."

"Wow!" exclaimed Mona. "What a terrific idea. But I still don't get what all the slogans mean. 'Cure all your troubles with Vitamin C'? and 'Vote for Christie, she's got the connections'? What's that all about, anyway?"

Christie felt emotion rising inside her like steam in a teakettle, and she opened her mouth to answer when Katie cut her off.

"Save your big speeches for later, Christie," said Katie.

Jana glanced nervously at Christie. "You see, Mona, we thought it would be great to have a class president who . . . well . . . sort of had an in with the teachers and with Mr. Bell."

"I get it," said Alexis. "Because Christie's mom is principal of Mark Twain and all the teachers know who she is, they would probably listen to her if she went to them and asked a big favor for our class. Pretty smart."

"You've got to help spread the word," said Melanie. "We can't exactly put all that on our posters, but once kids understand the idea, every time they see a poster they'll remember. Christie will have it made."

"Listen, you guys," said Christie. She couldn't stand being quiet any longer. She felt depressed and out of control. It was like being washed along by a huge wave. "I said I'd run for president, but I *never* said I'd ask for special favors if I got elected. If you want me to keep my promise and run, you'd better help me come up with a platform that I can live with."

Nobody said anything for a moment. Finally Melanie collected all the finished posters and called everybody to order. "Okay. We need to come up with a platform that Christie likes, and we need to do it now so that we can give it to Curtis tomorrow. I'll write," she said, pulling a pad of paper out of her backpack. "You talk."

"Melanie didn't like my ideas about women's lib," said Katie after everyone had stared at the floor and thought for a moment. "What about law and order? There's too much rowdiness and pushing in the halls."

"That's right," agreed Sara. "And Clarence Marshall is one of the worst."

"True," Jana joined in. "And what about a school mascot costume? We could try to get the school to buy an Indian outfit for the Wakeman Warriors, and someone could wear it to the pep rallies and in parades and do Indian dances at all the games."

"Great idea!" squealed Beth. "And I get to wear it first."

"Dummy," said Katie. "There would have to be competition to wear it. But it's a great idea."

"And what about more school dances?" chirped Melanie. "Just think, I'd have more chances to dance with Scott and Shane."

"And plays," added Beth. "We need more school plays and talent contests. Things like that."

"Wait a minute," cried Melanie. "I can't write that fast."

"I've got another idea," said Lisa. "From now on, let's all wear orange tops. People will notice, and we'll tell them it's for vitamin C, which is Christie's symbol, and ask them to vote for her."

"I thought I told you that I wouldn't run as someone who's going to cure everybody's troubles," Christie huffed.

"But you can't drop the symbol now," argued Alexis. "Everybody has seen it and knows it is you."

"That's true," piped up Mona. "But maybe we can just say that Christie is wholesome and sunny like vitamin C and that voting for her will make you feel good!"

"Terrific idea. We're on a roll now," shouted Katie.

Christie sat listening to her friends come up with ideas. They were so excited. And the new way of using vitamin C and oranges as her symbol was great. She knew that it ought to make her feel better, and she wished she could join in on all the planning, but she couldn't. They were talking about her, but it was almost as if she weren't even there.

CHAPTER

7

*A*fter dinner Christie moped around her room and tried to get ready for the next day at school. She placed the stickers for the lockers in her backpack along with her books and Melanie's notes for her interview with Curtis. She didn't feel like studying while she waited for Jon to come for the first tutoring session, so she opened a magazine and there, facing up at her like some kind of magic, was an advertisement for a Hawaiian vacation. Wouldn't it be great to go to an island in the South Pacific and do nothing?

The thought brought a smile to her face. What if she were stranded on a South Sea island with Jon Smith? Wouldn't that be great? They could lie in the sun and swim and do exactly what they wanted to. It made her feel dreamy. It would be nice if there was a Bumpers on the island so they could eat hamburgers instead of yucky fish. She giggled, but then her smile faded. Fat chance, she thought. Right now Jon doesn't even like me.

"Christie, there's someone here to see you," her father called.

She hadn't heard the door chimes, and she jumped up and quickly ran a brush through her hair. She grabbed her math book, drew in a deep breath, then walked into the living room. There, with her mother hovering around him and her father grinning at him, stood Jon Smith, books under his arm and looking totally miserable.

"We watch your mother on TV all the time," Mrs. Winchell was saying.

"Since your father is a sports director, I was wondering if he plays tennis?" asked her dad. "I'd like to talk to him about Christie's game sometime."

Christie cringed. "Hi," she said, forcing a big smile. This was definitely not the way to make friends with him. She guessed her chances of their ever dating had just dropped to minus ten.

"Hello," he answered. He looked as if he would rather be someplace else. Anyplace else. That South Sea island maybe, or even the North Pole. But certainly not with her.

She led him into the kitchen. "I guess we'd better study in here."

"It's up to you," he said coldly.

Christie shivered. This could turn out to be the worst evening of her life.

Opening her book, she asked, "What chapter are you on?"

"The class is on chapter five. I'm on chapter one," he muttered without opening his own book.

"Well, why don't we look at your assignments. Maybe I can tell where you need help."

He pulled out a rumpled sheaf of papers and shoved them across the table toward her. They were filled with scrawled numbers, a lot of which had been crossed out, and the margins were all marked up with doodles and scribbles. He certainly had not had his mind on math when he did them.

Biting her lower lip, Christie sorted the papers in what seemed to be the correct order. She didn't know what to say. She had always been taught that you should preface criticism by saying something good, but she couldn't see anything good about his homework. He hadn't even tried. Stalling for time, Christie faked interest in some problems on one page, but it was no use.

"I guess, maybe, we should start at the beginning," she said, drawing up her courage and trying to be businesslike.

"Whatever you say," he snapped.

Christie bristled. How dare he act as if she were the cause of his troubles? She was tired and had people all over her wanting her to do this and do that, and now he was acting as if she were helping him because she had nothing else to do.

"Hey, look! I didn't ask for this job," she said hotly. "I've got enough things to do without tutoring someone who doesn't want to be helped." That should do it, she thought. He not only won't ask me out, he'll be my enemy for life. He'll probably get up and walk right out of here.

"Well, you don't have to look as if you're enjoying it so much. How much money are my dad and mom paying you, anyway?"

Christie was stunned. "Paying me? I'm doing it because Mr. Bell asked me to."

He looked at her with raised eyebrows. "Come on. Who are you trying to kid? You're just like everybody else. You're doing it because you want to be able to say you know Chip Smith and Marge Whitworth."

"Think whatever you want to," Christie huffed. "But you heard Mr. Bell call me to his office. Believe it or not, I didn't know anything about it before then."

He scowled at her again, and she could read his thoughts as surely as if he were writing them down on paper. He still doesn't believe me, and on top of that, he doesn't like me one bit. Well, so what! she thought as anger and embarrassment flushed her face. He's so conceited that I don't like him either.

"We'd better get to work," she said, struggling to keep her composure. "The first thing you need to understand about equations is that the sum of the items on both sides of the equal sign have to be the same."

For the next hour Christie kept her eyes lowered, looking only at the math book and not at Jon. She went through the examples in lesson one and explained the principles behind them, trying as hard as she could to keep her mind strictly on math and refusing to think about Jon's mistaken opinion of her or how she'd blown any chance of his ever liking her. A couple of times she asked if he understood what she was talking about, and he mumbled something that she took as yes.

Finally the hour was over and Jon left without so much as a thank-you. The instant he was gone she raced upstairs to her room, not turning on the light but going to the window instead. In the glow of the streetlight she watched Jon mount his bicycle and ride away down the quiet street. When he was out of sight, she sighed and turned away. She couldn't remember when she had felt so mixed up. Part of her was angry. How dare he accuse her of taking money from his parents? Or them of bribing someone to help him, for that matter. But another part of her felt sad. Jon was mad at the world, and he seemed determined to take some of it out on her. She had hoped that they could at least be friends, but now she could see that it would never happen.

CHAPTER

8

"How did tutoring Jon go last night?" asked Jana as she caught up with Christie at the gate to the school ground.

Christie made a face. "It started out terrible and went downhill from there. He thought I had volunteered to tutor him just to meet his famous parents and get my kicks telling the world he's stupid. *Which*—by the way—he isn't. I told him Mr. Bell talked me into it. But did he believe me? Of course not!"

"It doesn't sound as if he asked you out."

"Are you kidding? He isn't even speaking to me. Grunting now and then when I asked him if he understands a problem, but speaking to me? Definitely not."

Jana looked at Christie sympathetically. "Gee. That's too bad. When do you tutor him again?"

"Tonight, after supper, but *boy*, do I dread it. I'm not sure I want to face him after last night."

"Listen, Christie. He's the one with the problem, not you. You don't have anything to be embarrassed about."

Christie smiled gratefully at Jana. She was right, of course, Christie told herself. She had daydreamed that he would be as much fun to be with as he was cute, but that dream had been blown away for good last night. But that wasn't going to make it any easier to tutor him again, just the same.

"Did you bring your stickers?" asked Jana as they hurried toward Melanie, Beth, and Katie, who were waiting for them at their spot by the fence.

"Got 'em right here," Christie said, patting her notebook.

"What took you guys so long?" asked Melanie. She and the others had their arms full of the big orange posters. Melanie had on an orange T-shirt; Beth, a pullover with orange stripes; Katie, orange ankle warmers; Jana, an orange shirt; and Christie had found an orange scarf to wear around her neck. They all wore stickers that said: VOTE FOR CHRISTIE WINCHELL—7TH-GRADE CLASS PRESIDENT.

"So how was tutoring Jon Smith last night?" asked Beth as they hurried toward the building.

Christie sighed and told her story all over again, emphasizing how rude he had been.

"Wow. That's too bad," said Melanie. "Maybe running for class president will help take your mind off of him."

Christie chuckled. Leave it to Melanie to think of my campaign that way, she thought. And by the time the friends were scurrying through the halls laughing and taping up the posters, her unhappy mood was gone.

Even though the walls were becoming cluttered with signs for candidates from all the classes, Christie had to admit that hers were attention-getters. The bright orange stood out against the soft beige walls and contrasted with the other posters.

Next, each of them put stickers on all the locker doors they had missed the day before and slapped new ones all over the doors of Laura McCall's, Funny Hawthorne's, Tammy Lucero's, and Melissa McConnell's lockers until they were nearly covered. Melanie put another sticker on Shane's and Garrett Boldt's lockers, "for good measure," she explained. Then they stuck them on drinking fountains, and Jana took a handful to put on the mirrors in the girls' bathrooms.

"I wish I could see Laura's and her friends' faces when they see their lockers," Beth said with a laugh when they were finished.

"She'll blow her stack," said Jana.

"I wonder if she'll make the others scrape them off," mused Katie. "You know she's supposed to make them do things to stay friends with her."

"I'll bet she's got a whip that she uses on them," Beth added, pretending to snap a big whip like an animal trainer. They all laughed and cowered in front of her as if she were using it on them.

"You know," said Christie. "I haven't seen any posters for Melissa yet." It bothered her. She had expected The Fantastic Foursome to be putting them up everywhere.

"You're right," answered Jana. "They've got to be planning something. I wonder what?"

She looked quizzically at her friends, but they all shook their heads.

Christie noticed Curtis Trowbridge sitting with Whitney Larkin at a table near the door as she went into study hall. Christie frowned. Whitney had gone to Copper Beach Elementary, but she didn't have very many friends. Nobody liked her because she was an absolute genius, and she made everybody uncomfortable by knowing the answers all the time. Not only that, Whitney had skipped sixth grade this year and had gone straight from fifth to junior high. Everybody said she was a baby.

"Hi, Curtis," said Christie, sitting down next to him.

"Hi," he said, looking up and smiling. "Have you met Whitney?"

They exchanged hellos, and Christie started to talk about her platform, but Curtis broke in.

"You know, Whitney is a superb student. She's made all A's every class she has ever been in, haven't you, Whitney?"

Whitney gave a little smile and nodded.

"That's nice. Curtis, I—"

"And she knows a great deal about computers, I might add. As a matter of fact, she and I have started networking together."

That sounds really romantic, thought Christie, as she tried to continue. "Curtis—"

"You wouldn't believe the software she and some of the kids from Copper Beach have. Why, it's mind expanding."

Christie couldn't believe what she was hearing. Curtis Trowbridge was raving over someone besides Jana Morgan. Curtis had had a crush on Jana since third grade, and he used to follow her around like a little lost puppy.

Christie looked at Whitney closer. While she wasn't in Taffy Sinclair's or Laura McCall's league, she wasn't bad looking. Christie had to admit that she looked just right for Curtis.

"Curtis!" Christie said firmly. "You asked me about my platform for the election to put in the article you're writing for the *Sig*, and I want to give it to you."

"Oh, uh . . . yes. The platform. Do you have it written out?"

"Here it is," she said, taking it from her notebook.

"Hmmm. Better food in the cafeteria. That would get you votes except Melissa McConnell has that one, too. Stop running in the halls. I'll bet Katie Shannon came up with that one. You'll lose Clarence Marshall's vote, if you care. Hmmm. More dances, something for the populace. Probably Melanie's idea, and more plays is Beth's. Hey, this is a good one. A costume for a school mascot. Melissa doesn't have that one. Hers are mostly prissy things, like getting rid of the gum tree. But don't forget, she's supposed to be a perfectionist."

"Getting rid of the gum tree?" Christie said so loudly that the study hall monitor frowned at her. "She can't do that. It's a Wacko tradition."

Curtis shrugged. "She says it's messy, it's unsanitary, and it's harmful to the tree. She wants a trash can with a plastic liner put by the front door."

Christie made a face, thinking about how Mr. Bell objected to chewing gum in the classroom and how the students had dubbed the tree beside the front door to the school "the gum tree" and stuck their gum on its bark every morning when the bell rang. "Leave it to Melissa," she grumbled.

"You know there's not much difference in your platforms," Curtis mused, looking down the list. "You'll get the Mark Twain vote and Melissa will get the Riverfield vote, and that makes you just about even. But why should someone like Whitney from Copper Beach vote for you?"

His question stopped Christie cold. She didn't know why someone from Copper Beach should vote for her instead of Melissa, and she said so.

"You've got to have something special to attract their attention," he said. "I'll vote for you, but Whitney has introduced me to a lot of kids who went to Copper Beach, and they don't care which one of you is elected."

Christie darted a quick glance at Whitney, who raised her head briefly from some problems she was working, gave Christie a vacant look, and went back to what she was doing. Curtis is absolutely right, thought Christie. Whoever gets the Copper Beach vote will win the election.

Christie was already at their table when the others came into the cafeteria.

"Hey, why so glum?" asked Jana. "I've seen a lot of kids looking at your posters."

"Yeah. But did you see the ones Melissa and her friends put up? They're good, too." Christie had seen them all over the school. The Fantastic Foursome must have put them up between classes. They were painted the colors of the rainbow and stood out brightly.

"Well, I think ours are better," pouted Beth.

"Maybe so," said Christie. "But I was talking to Curtis, and he said my platform isn't much different from Melissa's. He said we'd both get the votes of the kids from our own elementary schools, but then he asked why someone from Copper Beach would vote for me. He's been hanging around Whitney Larkin and knows a lot of them. I didn't know what to say to him. He's right, you know."

Gloom settled over The Fabulous Five as they thought about what Christie had said.

"What are *they* doing now?" Jana asked, looking toward the table where The Fantastic Foursome sat.

Laura and her friends had gotten up and were smiling their biggest smiles as everyone in the cafeteria watched them head for the open space near the serving line. The chatter of kids' talking faded as Laura, Tammy, and Funny positioned themselves behind Melissa and stood quietly for a moment. Then they burst into song.

> *"Melissa McConnell is the one for you.*
> *She'll make things happen we tell you true.*
> *If you want a president who'll be true blue,*
> *Vote for Melissa, that's what you should do.*
>
> *Vote for Melissa, put her to the test.*
> *Don't take a chance and please don't guess.*
> *Vote for Melissa over all the rest.*
> *Vote for Melissa if you care to*
> *   ELECT THE VERY BEST!"*

They ended their performance down on one knee with their arms open wide and big grins on their faces. The kids in the cafeteria went wild and started cheering and applauding. Christie could hear Clarence Marshall yelling, "RIGHT ON!" The noise went on for ten minutes before the teachers could get them to quiet down.

Melissa smiled broadly at everyone in the room and waved as if she were running for president of the United States.

Laura McCall was looking at The Fabulous Five, wearing a knowing smile, as Curtis Trowbridge leaned over from the next table where he was sitting with Whitney and some Copper Beach kids.

"Now that's different," he said, not even bothering to conceal his enthusiasm. "It got everybody's attention."

"Be at my house after school," Jana said to her friends with a look of grim determination on her face.

CHAPTER

9

"Okay. What are we going to do?" Jana asked her glum-faced friends as they sat around her kitchen table. "That stunt Laura, Melissa, Tammy, and Funny pulled in the cafeteria got everyone's attention. All I heard in my afternoon classes was how great it was."

"Well, Funny Hawthorne is supposed to be your friend," said Katie. "Why didn't she tell you they were going to do it?"

Christie saw Jana look with frustration at Katie. "You don't really expect her to tell me everything they're doing, do you? They're still her friends, too, you know."

"Arguing isn't going to solve anything," said Christie. "You guys put my name in for·president so it's up to you to think of some way to get me elected, *if* you're serious."

Katie looked at Jana. "I'm sorry. I just hate to see that witch Laura show off." Jana smiled understandingly.

"Look," said Melanie. "We've got to come up with something more spectacular than their silly little song. Something that will make people think about Christie more."

"Like what?" asked Katie.

"Listen, guys," Beth said excitedly. "I think you've just hit it. You said 'spectacular,' right? Get people's attention, right? Okay, Christie, listen up. You need to be more dramatic. Get some flash—"

Christie opened her mouth to protest when Melanie broke in. "Christie Winchell, don't listen to her! Didn't I tell you that boys make up half the class? What you need to do is go after the *boy vote*!"

"Melanie's right about one thing," Beth interrupted. "Boys are only half the class and half the vote. But if you could grab the spotlight away from Melissa and The Fantastic Foursome, you could get *all* the vote."

Melanie let out an exasperated sigh. "I could give you private flirting lessons. Or if you didn't want to do that, I could loan you my magazine with the seven tips for flirting in it."

Christie listened to the arguments lobbing back and forth like a tennis ball. Here they go again, she thought, planning my campaign as if I had nothing to do with it. At that moment something occurred to her. She smiled and held up her hand for silence.

"I have a better idea for getting everybody's attention," she said quietly. "It's dramatic and it could bring in both the boy vote *and* the girl vote. And best of all, it's something we've already thought of."

This time when Jon Smith rang the doorbell, Christie was ready and answered it before either of her parents could get up.

"Come in," she said coolly. She had promised herself that she wouldn't get into a fight with him again tonight, but at the same time she wasn't going to let him think that she cared what he thought of her either.

"Thanks," he said almost pleasantly.

As she led him to the kitchen, she wondered what he was up to. He had been so hostile the night before. Maybe he's trying to soften me up for the kill, she thought, and shivered.

Sitting down at the table and opening her book, she avoided looking at him. "Did you redo your homework for chapter one?" she asked.

He didn't answer. Instead he handed her a paper that was covered with neatly written problems. Without meaning to she glanced up at him and smiled. "Hey, these look better."

She skimmed the problems, making a check mark beside the ones that were wrong. He had missed only three out of twenty. That wasn't bad at all. She started to tell him so, but her anger with him held her back. Instead, she handed the homework back to him and turned to the next chapter.

"I think you're ready to move on," she said crisply.

"You *are* helping me just because Mr. Bell asked you to," Jon said. "I checked you out."

"You checked me out!" cried Christie, raising her blazing eyes to look straight at him. "What do you mean, you checked me out?"

"I asked my parents," he said matter-of-factly. "They said they called Mr. Bell and asked him to find a math tutor for me, and he called them later and said he had asked you to do it."

"So?" she challenged.

"Like I said yesterday, I thought you were doing it because you knew who my parents are. Lots of kids try to butter me up just to get to meet them. It happens all the time."

Christie bit her lower lip and shifted self-consciously in her chair. He was apologizing—sort of—and she knew she should forget her anger and accept.

"Don't take this wrong," he went on, "but I always thought that you were conceited."

Christie's eyes blazed at him again, but he held up a hand and smiled. "Whoa. Let me finish. Everyone knows that you make all A's and that you're running for class president. Besides that, Mr. Bell and the teachers all know you. I've seen them speak to you in the halls. I thought you just wanted to tutor me for the kicks."

This time she was able to return his smile. In fact, she felt such a rush of relief that she almost laughed out loud. "I make A's because my parents want me to, and I guess I want to, too. And my friends put my name in for class president. Believe me, if I could get out of it, I would. As far as Mr. Bell and the teachers go, it's just like your problem. My mom is principal of Mark Twain Elementary, and everybody at Wacko Junior High thinks that I have an in with all the teachers. I can't help it if they all know me."

He gave her a crooked grin. "Do you have any idea how many kids in this school have started their own rock bands and want me to use my influence with my parents to get them on television? I guess we both have the same kind of problem. Let's start over, okay? I promise not to be such a pain."

Christie looked into his smiling brown eyes. He seemed like a whole new Jon Smith now. He was suddenly more relaxed, and the way he looked at her told her that he meant what he said. Christie smiled back. It was going to be hard to concentrate on chapter two.

"We can get them," said Jana when they met at the fence the next morning. She could hardly contain her excitement. "Christie's idea was terrific. I talked to Mom and she called one of the grocers that advertises in her classified ads. He says we can have the oranges for a really good price, and he'll even have one of his trucks drop them off."

"Great," said Melanie, jumping up and down.

"Fantastic," said Katie.

"Super," said Beth.

Christie didn't say anything. In fact, she barely heard what they were saying. She couldn't get Jon out of her mind or the talk they had had last night.

"Earth to Christie, Earth to Christie," Beth sang, cupping a hand around Christie's ear. "Come in, Christie."

Christie blinked. "Sorry, guys. I was thinking about something else," she said. She could feel a blush creeping up her neck.

"Uh-oh," said Katie. "Tutoring must have gone a little better last night."

This time Christie was sure she was blushing. Nodding, she said, "Lots better. I think he even likes me— a little bit."

Her friends started cheering and asking a million questions. Finally Jana got everyone's attention back to the campaign and preparing the oranges to be handed out the next day.

"We can all get together after school today and put the stickers on them," she continued.

"VOTE FOR VITAMIN C! A DAY WITHOUT CHRISTIE IS LIKE A DAY WITHOUT SUN- SHINE," chirped Beth. "It's a *super* slogan. Look out Fantastic Foursome! Here come The Fabulous Five."

They all cheered, and Christie was glad the subject had changed.

"And I brought the stickers for the boys," said Katie.

"I talked to Scott last night, and he said he'd be glad to talk to Randy and Keith and all the rest of the football players," said Melanie.

"Did he say if the coach would let the players put the stickers on their helmets?" asked Katie.

"He said he thought it would be okay."

"What about the tape we recorded last night? Did you bring it?" Jana asked Melanie.

"Yes. And I called Bumpers and talked to Mr. Matson, and he said we could play it over the sound system."

Christie watched her friends having fun as they planned what they were going to do to beat Melissa. They had come up with the ideas for stickers on the football helmets at Saturday's game against Black Rock Junior High and the tape to be played at Bumpers after she had suggested the oranges.

She wished that she could feel as cheerful about all of it as they did.

It was Thursday so *The Wakeman Smoke Signal* was handed out in homeroom, just as Christie knew it would be. She quickly skimmed Curtis's article on the seventh-grade candidates and saw that he had been right. Her platform and Melissa's were an awfully lot alike. As much as she didn't want to be president, she couldn't let Melissa beat her. Those oranges have just got to do the trick, she thought, crossing and uncrossing her fingers three times for luck.

CHAPTER

10

*C*hristie and her friends rushed to Bumpers as soon as school was out and gave the tape to Mr. Matson. "You understand that if I play this for you, I've got to do the same for anyone else who is running for an office. I've got to give them equal time," he said, smiling.

"That's okay," said Melanie. Jana, Christie, Katie, and Beth nodded in agreement. "It's still best to be first."

"Okay. Just give me a signal when you want me to play it."

They rushed to get an empty booth.

Shortly Bumpers started filling up, but when Christie looked around for Jon, she didn't see him anywhere. She couldn't help being a little nervous about what he would think when he heard her tape.

When Melanie saw Scott, Randy, and Keith coming in from football practice, she waved to them, and they came over.

"Did you talk to the coach about the stickers?" Melanie asked Scott.

"No. I don't think it will be a problem, though. We'll wait until halftime and put the stickers on before we come out."

"Is everyone keeping it a secret?" she asked.

"Yep," he said, crossing his heart. The boys said good-bye and wandered off to talk to Tony Sanchez and Bill Soliday, who were standing at the counter placing an order for food.

"Oh, look. Here comes the head duck and her little ducklings," said Katie.

Christie turned to see Laura McCall walking in as if she owned the place. Following behind her were Funny, Melissa, and Tammy. They do kind of look like a mother duck and her little ducklings, she thought.

"I wish you wouldn't say bad things about *all* of them," said Jana. "Funny Hawthorne is nice."

"Sorry," said Katie. "We know you like her. But it looked so weird."

"Hey, there's Shane. I wonder who he's going to vote for," Melanie said, stretching and waving at him. "Shane! Shane!"

"Melanie! Can't you control yourself?" snapped

Katie, putting her hand over her eyes in embarrassment at Melanie's yelling.

Shane saw them and headed their way.

"Hi, girls," he said, flashing his handsome smile. Christie thought that Melanie was right—he did look like River Phoenix. Melanie was so thrilled that he had smiled at her that she looked as if she were going to leap out of her seat at him.

"Hey, Christie. I see you're running for class president. Lots of luck," he said.

"Oh, Shane. Who are you going to vote for?" Melanie blurted. "Christie or Melissa?" The five of them looked at him with anticipation.

He glanced from face to face and a slow smile came to his lips. "Laura asked me the same question. And do you know what I told her?"

"What?" asked Melanie, bouncing up and down in her seat.

"I told her that tonight I'd ask Igor who I should vote for and let everybody know tomorrow."

"You didn't," said Jana, giggling.

"Yes, I did. I always consult my pet iguana before I make an important decision. And so it's fair to everyone, I'll tell here at Bumpers tomorrow after school."

"Oh, you rat!" squealed Melanie. "Tell us now," she begged. "Please, please!"

"You're asking me not to talk to Igor first?" He raised his eyebrows in fake surprise and then laughed coolly. "Hey, I've got to live with him."

"It would be great if he'd vote for Christie," said Beth after Shane had left. "A lot of the Riverfield kids would vote for her, too, if he would."

"Do you suppose there's a chance he *will* vote for Christie?" asked Katie.

"I don't know," answered Jana. "He's pretty independent."

"I can't stand to wait until tomorrow to find out," said Melanie. "I'm going to call him tonight and see if I can talk him into telling me."

"Lots of luck," said Christie. "He's having too much fun."

"It looks as if everybody's here. Should we have Mr. Matson play the tape?" asked Melanie.

Christie had the sudden impulse to say no. She was getting pulled deeper and deeper into this election campaign, and the tape might be the thing that would make her the winner. Just then Jon's face flashed into her mind again. It had been comforting in a way to know that another person had to deal with pressure, too. But his way of dealing with it seemed to be by copping out. She couldn't do that. Not in a million years.

"Okay," she said. "Let's play the tape."

All five of them waved to get Mr. Matson's attention. He returned the wave and disappeared into the back room.

A few seconds later the music that had been playing stopped in mid-song. Some of the kids turned and looked curiously at the old-time Wurlitzer jukebox.

Then over the speakers came Beth's voice:

"A day without Christie is like a day without sunshine. Christie Winchell stands for . . . MORE SCHOOL DANCES . . ."

The recording hesitated, and The Fabulous Five started clapping and cheering. Then Lisa Snow, Alexis Duvall, and other kids from Mark Twain joined in.

"Christie Winchell stands for . . . A SCHOOL INDIAN COSTUME FOR A MASCOT AT ALL THE GAMES."

The cheers from the Mark Twain kids sounded louder this time. Some of the Riverfield kids booed.

"Christie Winchell stands for . . . MORE SCHOOL PLAYS."

The cheers and boos were much louder from both sides. Christie saw Laura looking furious and switching the tail of her long braid like a cat.

"VOTE FOR CHRISTIE WINCHELL FOR SEVENTH-GRADE CLASS PRESIDENT! SHE CAN MAKE IT HAPPEN!"

cried Beth's voice over the speakers.

Christie blushed as the Mark Twain kids came up to her to congratulate her on the recording. Between them she saw Jon Smith sitting in a booth in a far corner with some other boys from Copper Beach. He was looking at her, and she couldn't help wondering what he was thinking.

"My gosh, I've never seen so many oranges in my life," said Katie as the five friends stood in Jana's kitchen. They had giggled all the way to Jana's apartment from Bumpers. Laura had really looked mad after the recording had played.

There were oranges in mesh bags on the counters, loose oranges that Jana had dumped onto the table, and boxes of oranges on the floor. One orange rolled off the table and landed on Beth's foot. They were surrounded by oranges.

"Okay. If we're going to get all of these oranges done, we'd better get started. The one who works fastest gets to eat one!" cried Melanie. "Who wants to wipe oranges, who wants to make stickers, and who wants to stick them on?"

"Me! I'll make stickers," shouted Beth.

"I'll make stickers, too," cried Katie.

"I'll stick them on," said Jana.

"I'll take them out of the bags and boxes and put them back in," said Melanie. "What about you, Christie?"

Christie sighed and looked at the mountains of oranges. "I guess I'll wipe them," she offered halfheartedly.

They began laughing and chattering as they wrote "CURE ALL YOUR TROUBLES WITH VITAMIN C—VOTE FOR CHRISTIE WINCHELL" on stickers, peeled off the backing, and stuck them on the oranges, then put them back into the bags and boxes. All of them laughed except Christie. She couldn't get the look on Jon's face out of her mind. The one he'd had after her campaign tape had played at Bumpers.

CHAPTER

11

*J*on had redone his homework for chapters two, three, and four and gotten nearly all the problems correct. Christie was amazed at how accurate and neat his papers were, and he smiled proudly when she told him so.

"It's because of your help," he said. "You're a good teacher." Then he changed the subject.

"I was at Bumpers this afternoon when you played the recording. It really went over big. You probably have a good chance of being elected class president."

Christie looked down. The tape *had* gone over well, and it had been exciting when the kids were all congratulating her. But it didn't change anything. After the fun of planning the campaign with her friends was all over, if she won, she would be president.

"You really don't want to be class president, do you?" he asked as if he had read her mind.

She shook her head without saying anything.

"Why are you running, then?" he asked.

"My friends want me to. I promised them I'd try. And my parents would be disappointed, too, if I dropped out of the election."

"That's the difference between the two of us, I guess," he said, frowning. "You try to satisfy everyone, and I don't try to satisfy anyone, because I know I can't."

"But you can do well when you really want to," she insisted. "Look at how fast you're catching up in math."

He smiled at her. "For some reason I feel like trying now. Maybe you *shouldn't* try so hard. I don't mean that you should be like me or make bad grades. I mean, just don't do everything everyone wants you to."

"I don't know," she answered. "I've done it all my life."

"Don't get me wrong," he added quickly. "It's just that you're important, too. If you keep being the person everybody else thinks you should be, you'll never find out who the real Christie is."

"And if you keep copping out," she added, looking deep into his eyes, "you'll never know how special you can be."

Neither of them said anything for a minute. Then Jon grinned. "What's that old saying about a happy medium?" he asked. "Maybe we should both look for that."

"It's a deal," said Christie.

She poured them each a soda, and they settled down at the table to work on math. Jon was almost caught up now. Christie was proud of his progress, but she also dreaded for the tutoring sessions to end. Especially now that things were going so well between them.

When the lesson was finished, Jon closed his book and started to get up from the table, but for some reason he sat back down. Christie was puzzled by the serious look on his face, and then surprised when he put his hand on top of hers. It made her feel tingly all over.

"You've helped me a lot," he began. "Now I think I know how to help you."

"How?"

"By helping you get out of the elections."

"I don't know. Everyone is depending on me," she said with a sigh. "I can't just back out."

"What if someone besides you *or* Melissa won?" he asked.

She looked at him, not understanding. "But there's no one else running. No one from Copper Beach Elementary is."

"I've been thinking," he said. "What if there was a mystery candidate? Someone no one knew? That would get a lot of attention, wouldn't it?"

She looked at him blankly. "A mystery candidate?"

"Think about how excited everyone would get if all of a sudden there were posters for a candidate without a name. We could even make a tape like you did and ask Mr. Matson not to tell who made it."

"But who would the candidate be? Don't tell me that *you're* thinking of running now?"

He chuckled and raised his hands in protest. "Not me. I haven't figured out who it could be yet, but we've got until next Tuesday to come up with someone. And I promise you that it won't be a cop-out candidate, either. We'll find someone who'll do a good job."

"Do you mean to say that you want to campaign for someone and you don't even know who it is?" she asked incredulously.

"Sure. Why not? Are you game?"

Christie laughed. Coming up with a mystery candidate really sounded like fun. It just might work. And if it did . . .

"It's still early. If you could stay a little longer, we could plan our campaign," she said.

"Let's do it," he said, opening his notebook with a flourish. "Maybe our candidate, whoever it is, will go on to be the next president of the United States." They laughed together.

As Jon bent his head down over the notebook, Christie looked at him. He was a lot different from the first night he had come over to study. His eyes were twinkling and he was excited about what they were doing.

He looked so handsome with the lock of soft brown hair down on his forehead. She was happier being with him than she would ever be running for some dumb old school office. If this was what it meant to look for the happy medium, she was all for it.

CHAPTER

12

*C*hristie and Jon were waiting at the school doors when Mr. Bartosik, the head custodian, opened them early the next morning before any other students had arrived. After they dropped her bag of oranges off at her locker, they rushed through the empty halls to carry out their plan.

Mrs. Winchell had given them long rolls of newsprint that were left over from an art project at Mark Twain Elementary, and they had painted brightly colored banners for their mystery candidate on them, rolled them back up, and carried them to school. Now they were unrolling them again and taping them up in the hallway where everyone would see them.

Christie took a deep breath and crossed her fingers as she put up the last poster. "We can't back out now," she said.

"Good luck, mystery candidate, whoever you are!" Jon added with a laugh.

A little while later Christie hurried to The Fabulous Five's favorite spot by the fence to wait for her friends, and she had been standing there, fidgeting nervously, for nearly fifteen minutes before they arrived.

"Hi," called Melanie as she and Beth walked up, pulling a wagon full of oranges. "I bribed my little brother by promising him a double-scoop ice cream cone after school if he would let me borrow his wagon," she said brightly. Katie and Jana were right behind them, carrying their oranges in brown paper bags.

"Boy, I can't wait to see what Laura and her friends have planned for today," said Katie as they unloaded the fruit into their lockers. "You know she's not going to take yesterday without a fight."

"I couldn't forget the look on her face all last night," said Beth, giggling, as she stuffed a bag loaded with oranges on top of some books. "I even dreamed about her standing there flicking her braid. I woke up laughing."

"Well, I'll bet The Fantastic Foursome had a long meeting yesterday to figure out what to do next," said Katie.

"Maybe they'll sing that dumb little commercial in the cafeteria again," added Melanie.

"I don't know about that, but I'll bet they have a tape to play at Bumpers after school," said Jana. "What do you think, Christie?"

Christie smiled. "Oh, I'm sure we'll get some surprises today." Then to herself she added, If only you knew!

"If anyone hears about what they're up to, spread the word," said Katie. "Did you call Shane last night like you said you would?" she asked Melanie.

"Yes. And the rat wouldn't tell me who he's going to vote for. He said to be at Bumpers this afternoon and he'd tell everyone what Igor said."

They all laughed at the thought of Shane's talking to his pet iguana. All except Christie. Were they going to stand around talking forever? she wondered. She was dying to walk around the halls where the posters for the mystery candidate were hanging and see what kind of attention they were getting. But at the rate The Fabulous Five were moving, they would still be standing at their lockers when the first bell rang.

"Hey, look," whispered Jana. "There are Laura and the others. Let's keep an eye on them."

The halls were filling up as more and more kids arrived for school, so they were able to follow The Fantastic Foursome without being seen. Suddenly Laura and her friends stopped in the middle of the hall by the principal's office and stood looking at a poster. Melanie motioned the others to follow her, and they walked up trying to look as if they were just on their way to class.

Christie had to bite her lower lip to keep from giggling. The poster had a cutout of Vanna White standing by some hand-printed squares that looked like the ones on the *Wheel of Fortune* television show. The blocks were empty as if they were part of a puzzle. Underneath them was printed:

WHO IS THE MYSTERY CANDIDATE FOR 7TH-GRADE CLASS PRESIDENT?

Christie hoped everyone would realize that they were supposed to guess the name that went in the squares.

"Is this another one of your tricks?" Laura snapped at them. "If it is—well, you've got it right. It's a *mystery* why you put Christie up for class president."

"Yeah," said Tammy. "You would have been better off keeping the whole *thing* a mystery. Especially after Melissa wins." The four of them turned in unison and stomped off.

As they moved closer to see, Christie faked interest in the poster. She had to admit that she and Jon had done a good job in the short time they had had the night before.

"If they didn't put it up, I wonder who did?" Jana thought out loud.

"You've got me," said Melanie.

Christie turned so that no one could see her face. She couldn't help feeling a mixture of guilt, over not being honest with her best friends, and glee, over the trick she and Jon had pulled off.

Just then Lisa Snow and Sara Sawyer came up behind them and stopped to look at the poster. "Who put that up?" Lisa asked.

"We don't know," answered Katie.

"Is it legal?" Sara asked.

"Sure," answered Katie. "You can write in anyone you want. You only have to get petitions signed if the candidate's name is going to be on the ballot."

Randy Kirwan and Scott Daly walked up and looked at the poster, too, and soon a crowd had gathered. Everyone started trying to guess the name of the mystery candidate. Christie listened and had a hard time keeping a straight face. What makes it even funnier, thought Christie, is that it's taped up next to one of Melissa's posters. One that says she wants to clean up the gum tree. How boring, compared to a mystery candidate.

"Maybe it's Whitney Larkin," offered someone in the crowd.

"Naw," said someone else. "There aren't enough letters."

"Hey, look," called Jana, who had walked down the hall a short way. "Here's another one." Christie followed as everyone rushed down to see.

This one said:

WHO DOES EVERYONE KNOW?
WHO KNOWS EVERYTHING
THAT'S GOING ON?
WHO DOES EVERYONE TRUST?
WHO WOULD MAKE THE BEST
7TH-GRADE CLASS PRESIDENT?
VOTE FOR THE MYSTERY
CANDIDATE
_____ ?

As the group of seventh-graders stared at the poster in silence, Christie had to bite her lip to keep from grinning.

When the bell rang signaling the start of seventh-grade lunch period, Christie raced to her locker and grabbed her lunch and her grocery bag of oranges. The bag was practically overflowing, and she balanced it carefully, clamping her chin down on the oranges on top to keep them from spilling onto the floor as she headed for the cafeteria.

She ignored curious stares as she made her way toward The Fabulous Five's regular table. Katie was already there with her oranges, and Jana and Beth were coming through the swinging doors behind Christie. That left Melanie, and she was a few minutes late because she had persuaded Mr. Bartosik to let her store the wagonload of oranges in the supply closet down the hall.

"That should do it," she said as she shoved the wagon under the table and sat down with a breathless sigh.

"Has anyone found out who put those posters up for the mystery candidate?" asked Jana, taking a bite of her cream cheese and jelly sandwich. "They're all over school."

Christie cringed at the mention of the mystery candidate. It was one thing to dream up the scheme with Jon and another to have to keep a straight face while her friends talked about it.

"No," grumbled Beth. "But I still think it was Laura and her friends."

"I don't think so," said Katie. "They really seem to be as confused as everyone else."

"I agree," said Jana. "There *is* someone else running. But who could it be?"

"Somebody who knows more people, the poster says," answered Melanie.

"And knows about everything that's going on," added Beth. "And someone people trust."

"That definitely leaves out Laura and her friends," snickered Katie.

"Come on, guys," said Christie, desperately trying to change the subject. "If we're going to pass these oranges out, we'd better get at it."

"Right," said Jana, "before Melissa and her friends sing their dumb little jingle again."

They cleared away their lunch bags and then began passing out oranges to all the seventh-graders. Christie took the outer rows of tables on the left side; Katie took the outer rows on the other side. Jana and Beth worked the next rows, and Melanie pulled her little brother's wagon up the center aisle.

"Gimme two!" shouted Clarence Marshall. Without even reading the stickers he began trying to juggle the oranges, but instead of catching them, they crashed down on his head. Everyone around him roared with laughter.

Soon kids all over the room were raising their hands and asking for oranges, and the girls were wading through the tables as fast as they could hand them out. Only Laura McCall and her friends refused them, sticking their noses into the air and turning away when Beth went by their table.

When Christie reached Jon, he was smiling. "What do your friends think of the posters for the mystery candidate?" he whispered.

Christie laughed. "It blew their minds. Wow! Have I been having trouble keeping a straight face."

"It's going to work," he assured her.

Christie nodded and handed him an orange. For an instant they both held it, looking at each other and smiling.

CHAPTER

13

*C*hristie and her friends were in a happy mood when they reached Bumpers after school. Laura and her friends had not done their little commercial for Melissa at lunchtime, and except for the appearance of the posters for the mystery candidate, the day was a total victory for The Fabulous Five—so far.

Christie was feeling especially optimistic, and she tried to act as if it were for the same reason as her friends. The truth was, she was so excited about the mystery candidate and all the attention the posters were getting that she could barely sit still in the booth.

"I can't wait for Shane to get here," said Melanie. "I just know he's going to vote for Christie."

"Maybe Igor told him to vote for the mystery candidate," suggested Christie.

Melanie looked at her and frowned.

"Everyone I talked to today was asking about the mystery candidate," said Jana. "Whoever it is has some pretty good posters, and everyone's dying to figure out who it is."

"I don't think it's fair," said Melanie. "Whoever it is should come out and say."

"I think it's really smart. I wish we had thought of it," responded Katie.

"Well, tomorrow when the football players come out in the second half of the game with Vitamin C stickers on their helmets, Christie will get some really good publicity," Melanie assured her.

"Has Scott ever asked the coach if it's okay to do that?" asked Beth.

"No, but he's not worried about it," said Melanie. She glanced toward the door and her eyes got big. "Oh, LOOK!" she squealed. "There's Shane. AND HE'S GOT IGOR WITH HIM!"

Like everyone else, Christie turned toward the door to see. Shane was standing in the entrance holding his iguana stretched along one arm and was gently stroking Igor's throat with his fingertips. Igor's tongue was darting out and his eyes blinked as if he were bored with all the attention.

Curtis Trowbridge rushed forward with his notebook as Shane carried Igor to the center of the room and set him down on the floor. All the kids gathered around to see as Curtis took notes furiously. Curtis doesn't miss anything, Christie thought.

Draped across Igor's back was a square of blue cloth with hand-lettered writing on both sides. Everyone pushed forward to see what it said. On each side it read:

IGOR FOR CLASS PRESIDENT

"What can I say?" said Shane. "He just felt that he was the best candidate. You can't argue with him. He won't listen." Everyone laughed.

While they were all fussing over Igor, Christie looked at Mr. Matson, who was behind the counter. She nodded, and he went into the back room to play the tape that Jon had given him.

When the music on the sound system stopped, everyone turned expectantly to listen.

"THIS IS YOUR MYSTERY CANDIDATE SPEAKING," came Jon's muffled voice. Christie put her hand over her mouth to hold in a giggle as she remembered how she and Jon had laughed when he had tried to disguise his voice last night. He had not only succeeded in hiding his own identity, but the voice was so muffled that you couldn't tell if it was a boy or a girl.

"WHO KNOWS THE MOST ABOUT WHAT'S GOING ON AT WACKO JUNIOR HIGH? WHO

KNOWS THE MOST KIDS FROM COPPER BEACH, RIVERFIELD, AND MARK TWAIN? WHO HAS PROVEN HE WILL WORK HARD FOR YOU?" Jon's voice paused to let the questions sink in. "ME, THAT'S WHO. YOUR MYSTERY CANDIDATE. WRITE IN MY NAME TUESDAY." Then, for effect, Jon gave what was supposed to be a mysterious laugh. Christie broke up.

"Who in the world was that?" asked Jana, looking at Christie.

"How should I know?" she answered quickly. "It just struck me funny."

"It may be funny," said Katie, "but he sure has everybody's interest, including mine. He's got to let everyone know who he is before Tuesday though, if he really wants people to vote for him."

"I think we're in trouble," said Melanie. "Even our oranges didn't get this much attention."

"And we'll be paying for them all year," moaned Beth. Then bolting up in her seat, she cried, "What's Laura doing?"

"ATTENTION EVERYONE!" Laura was standing and she had raised her hands for quiet. "I want you all to know that anyone who votes for Melissa McConnell next Tuesday is invited over to my house for a victory celebration Friday night. And you know how much fun that can be," she added slyly. She glanced toward the booth where Christie and her friends were sitting and her lip curled in a sneer.

* * *

"Can you believe that Laura is inviting everyone who votes for Melissa over to her house on Friday?" Christie shook her head in amazement as she and Jon talked over the things that had happened that day. They were sitting next to each other on her front porch.

"No. And I thought I'd fall out of my bumper car when Mr. Matson played that tape. You should have told me I sounded that funny last night when we were making it."

"I thought you knew from the way I kept giggling."

Jon tried to look serious, and his voice sounded solemn. "The only problem I see now is that Igor might split the vote and you'll still get elected." Then he burst out laughing. Christie was laughing so hard as well that tears ran down her cheeks.

Finally they got control of themselves, and Jon leaned back against the white porch pillar. He had shown Christie his finished homework when he arrived, and he had done it so well that their lesson time had been very short, and they had decided to sit on the porch for a while before he went home.

The only sound at the moment was an occasional chuckle from him or a giggle from her as they sat thinking about their day. Then Christie felt his arm reach around her, and she gladly gave in to his gentle pull and leaned against his shoulder.

She smiled dreamily to herself. She was having so much fun with him. It was almost better than she had imagined it would be. For the first time since she had started junior high, she felt relaxed, and she had forgotten the pressure of the election.

All of a sudden, since she and Jon had gotten to know each other, her troubles had seemed to roll off her shoulders. And Jon seemed more relaxed, too. The stiff jaw and tight lip he had before had now disappeared. He was laughing most of the time they were together. It felt so good. Then a thought came to her.

"I know of one more problem that we have besides Igor," she said, looking up into his face.

"What's that?" he asked, smiling at her.

"Who is the mystery candidate?"

"Oh, yeah. We haven't figured that out yet, have we?"

"No. And the elections are Tuesday."

"Who do we know who knows people from all three elementary schools, knows a lot about what's going on, whom everyone knows is a hard worker, and everyone would think was fair?" he asked.

Christie thought a moment. Then she sat up straight and said, "I know who that is, and so do you. I don't know why we didn't think of him sooner." Then, before Jon could ask any questions, she added mysteriously, "And I think that he just might agree to do it."

CHAPTER

14

"Quick! There they are," said Christie, pulling at Jon's hand. "If we hurry we can catch them." The crowd was milling through the stadium gate, and Christie and Jon threaded their way, trying to keep Curtis and Whitney in sight.

"This way," said Jon, once they had entered the stadium. "They're headed for the refreshment stand." Running hand in hand, they reached Curtis and Whitney as they were studying the menu board above the stand.

"Curtis, we need to talk to you," Christie said, stopping next to him.

"Sure," said Curtis, puffing up importantly and giving Whitney a sideways smile. "What can I do for you?"

He's showing off for Whitney, thought Christie. This is great! He's playing right into our hands.

"Jon and I have a *secret* proposition for you. One we hope you won't turn down."

Curtis raised an eyebrow and straightened his shoulders. "Only if Whitney can listen. We don't keep secrets from each other." He was holding Whitney's hand and he patted it affectionately.

"Why don't we move out of this crowd where we can talk privately," said Jon.

Curtis is really going for this, thought Christie as she watched him look in both directions and then rush to a spot by the stadium wall, pulling Whitney along with him.

When Christie and Jon reached him, he put his hand over his mouth and whispered, "Okay. Now what's this all about?"

"Well, you see, Curtis, we know who the mystery candidate is," Christie said.

Curtis and Whitney looked at each other. "*Who!?*" croaked Curtis.

"You," said Jon.

Curtis stared blankly at him.

"What do you mean precisely by 'you'?" questioned Whitney. "You can't really mean Curtis."

"Yes, we do. The mystery candidate is someone who knows kids from Copper Beach, Mark Twain, and Riverfield elementary schools, knows about everything that's going on, is someone everyone trusts, and is a hard worker," said Christie. "Who else could it be but you, Curtis?"

"Now wait a minute," said Curtis, raising his hands in protest. "I didn't put up all those posters or make that tape we heard in Bumpers."

"We know that," said Jon reassuringly. "But no one else does."

"Do you mean that you two did that?" Whitney's mouth dropped open, and she and Curtis looked like a pair of matched bookends in their surprise.

"Sure. We did it for you, Curtis. I'm not the right person for seventh-grade class president. And neither is Melissa," Christie added quickly. "Think about it," she continued. "You really do have friends from all the elementary schools."

"You're from Mark Twain, and Whitney's from Copper Beach," added Jon.

"No one knows more about what's going on around Wakeman than you do," said Christie.

"Everybody trusts you and you're a hard worker," Jon said, punctuating his words with a raised fist.

Christie took her cue and came in for the kill. "You know, Curtis, I've been noticing you at school lately. From your actions and the way you handle things, I'd have to say that I believe you could become a senator someday or maybe even president."

Curtis had been moving his head back and forth from Christie to Jon as they talked. Now he pulled himself up to his full height and looked at Whitney to see if she was listening. "Well . . . ," he said, "if you really think . . ." He seemed to be hesitating, but his eyes were glistening.

Christie knew they had their mystery candidate.

"OKAY!" Curtis's voice sounded like the crack of a whip. "How do you think we should proceed?"

"Did you two really put up all those posters and make that tape just for Curtis?" asked Whitney.

Christie and Jon smiled at each other.

CHAPTER

15

Christie saw Jana and Katie sitting in the cheering section at the same instant they saw her. She waved to her friends and took Jon's hand, heading up the stadium steps to join them.

"Hi," she said as they squeezed into the aisle. Jon hadn't gone home early enough the night before for her to be able to call her friends and tell them that she would be going to the ball game with him, and both Katie and Jana wore looks of total astonishment as Christie and Jon sat down. They gave her a thumbs-up victory sign as soon as Jon looked in another direction.

"Look," said Jana, pointing to Beth and Melanie standing on the sidelines with the other cheerleaders.

They were wearing their gold and cardinal-red uniforms. "Don't they look terrific?"

Melanie was talking to Darcy Holyfield, and Beth was shielding her eyes from the sun and looking up into the stands. When she saw them, she jumped up and down and waved her pom-pons at them. Laura McCall and Tammy Lucero were standing to one side, and Tammy had her hands cupped around Laura's ear, whispering. That gossip! thought Christie.

"Where's Randy?" she asked, looking toward the end zone where the Wakeman players were lined up in rows doing calisthenics.

"He's in front with Shane leading the exercises," said Jana.

Christie searched the crowd until she saw Curtis. He was coming up the stairs with Whitney and was stopping to talk to someone in nearly every aisle. She nudged Jon and nodded in Curtis's direction. Jon saw him and winked at her.

"Boy, don't you know what a mess you made?" came an angry voice from behind them. Christie turned to see who had made the remark. It was Melissa McConnell. She and Funny Hawthorne had taken seats in the next row up, and both were wearing Melissa's campaign ribbons in their hair.

"There are orange peelings all over school and the school ground, Christie Winchell," Melissa continued in a voice loud enough for everyone in the cheering section to hear. "Some of the boys were even throwing oranges at each other. And it's all your fault! I'm campaigning to clean up that awful unsanitary gum tree in front, and you're handing out *garbage*. I don't know why you think *you* should be elected."

Funny looked embarrassed.

"You're just mad because you didn't think of the oranges first," Katie shot back at her.

"Did you hear about the mystery candidate?" asked Richie Corrierro, who was sitting in front of them. "I'm glad there's no mystery candidate running for treasurer. I wouldn't have a chance."

"Who do you think it is?" asked Marcie Bee, who was sitting nearby. Instantly everyone seemed to forget about Melissa's angry accusations and started talking about the mystery candidate again. Christie looked at Jon, and they both had to turn away to keep from laughing.

"Oh, look. There go the team captains," cried Jana. Randy and Shane were walking out to the center of the field to meet the Black Rock captains. Randy called the toss of the coin and won and elected to receive the kickoff. Christie thought she had never seen Jana look so proud.

The teams were evenly matched, and they played hard. Randy threw passes and Scott and Shane ran and caught balls, but the Black Rock defense stopped them whenever they got near the goal line. The Wakeman defense was just as tough. Neither team was able to score in the first half, and both sides looked tired when they went to the dressing rooms at half-time.

Jana motioned Christie closer. She leaned sideways, and the two of them and Katie put their heads together.

"Wait until the team comes out again with the stickers on their helmets. It's the best publicity you've had so far, Christie. I'm just glad Laura and Tammy are down on the field where they can see them up close," Jana whispered and then giggled.

"Laura will absolutely boil," Katie whispered back. "I just wish we were closer so we could see her face."

Frowning, Christie sat back down again. In the excitement over persuading Curtis to be the mystery candidate, she had forgotten all about the stickers that the football team would wear when they returned to the field from the halftime break. Jana had been right about one thing, she thought. They would be terrific publicity—but for the wrong candidate. What she needed now was less publicity, not more. What would she do if Curtis announced that he was the mystery candidate and she won the election anyway?

She looked where he and Whitney were seated. Curtis was talking to everyone around him. He's a natural candidate, Christie thought. She had meant it when she told him she thought he would probably be a senator someday. Or maybe president. Besides, he had to start his career someplace, and Wacko Junior High was as good as any. Christie Winchell and Jon Smith, kingmakers, she thought, giggling to herself as she glanced quickly at Jon.

The players came back onto the field, and Christie looked hard at their helmets. On the back, as plain as could be, were the big orange stickers.

Richie Corrierro was the first to notice. "What's that on the back of the players' helmets?" he asked. Everyone leaned forward to see.

"What is that?" everyone started to ask.

Christie saw the cheerleaders turn to look at the players. Laura McCall froze as she stared at them, and then her fists went on her hips, and she huffed angrily over to Beth and Melanie and started shouting. Christie wished she could hear.

Christie could see the word being passed back from the kids who had seats near the field like a gigantic wave. Finally it reached where they were sitting.

"It says, VITAMIN C FOR SEVENTH-GRADE PRESIDENT!" shouted Richie, grinning at Christie. "That's a pretty slick way of advertising."

"Way to go, Christie!" shouted Mona Vaughn, waving her clenched fists.

"I can't believe it!" said Melissa, jumping to her feet. "First you pollute the school and now you pollute the football team!"

Christie ignored Melissa and tried to concentrate on the game. She didn't want to think about the stickers right now, and what they could mean to her campaign.

The teams went at each other again. Gradually Wakeman edged the ball toward the Black Rock goal line. Suddenly Christie saw Randy roll to the right and fake a pitchout to Scott.

What's he doing that for? she wondered. But then the Black Rock players went for Scott, and Randy cut back, splitting two defenders and crossing the goal line standing up. Shane kicked the extra point, and the green numbers on the scoreboard said: Wakeman seven, Visitors zero. The crowd went wild, and Christie and Jon hugged each other.

Wakeman lined up to kick off to Black Rock. Suddenly one of the officials blew his whistle and stopped the game. He walked over to one of the Wakeman players and looked at the back of his helmet.

"What's going on?" asked Jon. "What are the officials doing?"

The officials, in their white-and-black-striped shirts, had gone over to the Wakeman bench and were talking to Coach Bledsoe. The coach was looking back and forth between the officials and the players. He walked over to Scott and turned him around and looked at the back of his helmet. Throwing up his hands, he went back to the officials. The Wakeman crowd went silent, as if they were all holding their breath.

"Uh-oh," said Katie, clenching her teeth. "Scott should have asked the coach if it was okay to put the stickers on the back of the helmets."

"Oh, no," said Christie, turning to Jon. "What will the officials do to the players?"

"Make them take the stickers off. I hope that's all. There's not supposed to be any advertisement on the players. I guess they could make them forfeit the game."

"It'll be your fault if we lose, Christie Winchell," said Melissa from the next row. Christie turned and gave her a drop-dead look.

"It wasn't your idea," Katie said, putting her hand on Christie's knee. She looked worried.

Christie bit her lower lip. She couldn't believe the stickers with her name on them were causing all this trouble. On the bright side, they might damage her campaign and give the mystery candidate an even bigger edge. But what if they cost Wakeman the game? How could she live with that?

The officials huddled for some time and then went back to talk to Coach Bledsoe. The crowd had gotten so quiet, thought Christie, that you could hear a kernel of popcorn drop.

Jon squeezed her hand as the public address system crackled to life. "The Wakeman Warriors are penalized fifteen yards for illegal uniforms. The penalty will be assessed on the kickoff."

A giant "WHOOSH!" went up as the Wakeman spectators let out their collective breath. Christie leaned against Jon in relief. Then she watched the jubilant Wakeman players take the stickers off their helmets and go on to win the game fourteen to seven.

CHAPTER

16

*C*hristie walked into the school on Monday morning with the rest of The Fabulous Five. Her friends were all hyper about the election and her chances of becoming president, but Christie had something else on her mind—Curtis. What if he revealed that he was the mystery candidate too soon and blew the whole thing? She knew she would be nervous all day, especially when everyone saw the new posters. Would he be able to keep his mouth shut?

Jon, Curtis, Whitney, and she had gone to Curtis's house yesterday to make posters that said, MYSTERY CANDIDATE TO BE REVEALED AT BUMPERS MONDAY AFTER SCHOOL. It had been fun, and with all four of them working on Curtis's campaign, Christie had the feeling that it just might work, and she wouldn't be elected. Now she had her fingers crossed behind her back as they walked down the hall where kids were gathered around one of the posters that Curtis and Whitney had put up earlier that morning.

"Can you imagine the nerve?" Katie's voice sounded frantic. "Everyone will vote tomorrow morning in homeroom, and whoever this clown is, is going to wait until after school today to reveal his or her identity. Okay, guys. We've got to put on a big push for Christie while we still can."

"Right," agreed Jana. "We all have to talk to everyone we know today. We can't let this mystery candidate win."

"I'll talk to Scott and some of the other boys," said Melanie.

Katie looked at her with exasperation. "After your idea about putting stickers on the football helmets, I think you'd better be careful with the players."

"Well, if Scott had only checked with the coach like he was supposed to . . . ," Melanie pleaded.

"It doesn't matter now," said Jana. "What matters is getting Christie elected."

"Would it really be that bad if someone besides me or Melissa were to win?" asked Christie. She had been listening to their conversation and trying desperately to think of some way to discourage them. "I thought we were mostly interested in beating Melissa."

"That's true," said Beth. "But who knows who this mystery candidate really is. I mean, it could be someone worse than Melissa—like Taffy Sinclair, for instance."

"Or somebody gross like Clarence Marshall," said Melanie, wrinkling her nose.

"So, what if it's someone terrific?" offered Christie. "What if all the posters are right and this person is hardworking and popular and deserves to be president?"

"But we don't know that the mystery candidate is someone terrific," argued Jana, "and if it turns out to be someone horrible and you stop trying to win, Melissa will win for sure. She'll get all of Riverfield and then part of Mark Twain and Copper Beach. Your staying in is the only way the mystery candidate can have a chance."

"And don't forget all the kids who might vote for Melissa just to go to a party at Laura's," cautioned Katie. "You'd be letting everybody down if you let that happen."

Christie knew in her heart that Jana and Katie were right. She hadn't thought about it before, but she had to keep running to keep Melissa from getting votes. And if she backed out, everyone would think that she was afraid to run against Melissa. She wanted to find the happy medium, but just as always, things were out of control, and she was being swept along. Oh, Jon, she thought, I hope our plan works.

The after-school crowd at Bumpers was enormous. Christie, Jana, and Beth had to squeeze through the people at the door.

"Over here! Over here!" Melanie waved and shouted above the din from the booth where she and Katie were saving seats.

Christie looked around the room. Every booth and bumper car was packed, and kids were standing in the aisles. Jon was near the counter talking with Tony Sanchez and Bill Soliday, and Curtis and Whitney were on the other side of the room talking to Mandy McDermott and Darcy Holyfield.

Christie gulped. This was the big moment. She was frightened. What if she had been wrong about Curtis's being the best candidate? What if Curtis did something foolish in front of everyone? She would die.

Whitney looked at Christie and nodded slightly when kids finally stopped coming in the door. Then she walked over and said something to Mr. Matson. Christie looked nervously at Jon, and he gave her a reassuring smile. Then the music playing on the old Wurlitzer stopped.

Everyone turned to see what was going on. Suddenly, over the sound system came the blare of trumpets, and people looked at each other and snickered.

Christie cringed. *Oh, no*, she thought. Is Curtis going to make *too* big a deal out of this? Will everyone laugh?

At that moment Whitney stepped forward and waited calmly for everyone to stop talking.

"I have the honor and the pleasure," she spoke clearly and with pride in her voice, "to announce the name you have all been waiting to hear." She paused for effect.

"The name of the person whom we from Copper Beach and, I'm sure, you from Mark Twain and Riverfield all know and respect.

"The name of the seventh-grade person who has already made a name for himself at Wakeman.

"The name of the person who knows the most about what is happening at school.

"The name of the mystery candidate."

Kids started to applaud, but she held up her hand and the room got quiet again.

"The name of the NEXT PRESIDENT OF THE SEVENTH-GRADE CLASS OF WAKEMAN JUNIOR HIGH IS . . . CURTIS . . . ELWOOD . . . *TROWBRIDGE!*"

The room remained in stunned silence for a long moment. Christie's heart sank within her. It was worse than she could ever imagine. It seemed that nobody could believe that the mystery candidate was Curtis!

Finally, after what seemed like ages, Mandy and Darcy started whispering to each other. And then gradually other kids began talking and whispering until a buzz of voices filled the room, but no one was saying anything to Curtis, who stood beside Whitney with a look of horror growing on his face.

"CUR-TIS! CUR-TIS! CUR-TIS!" shouted Jon, raising his fist in the air each time he said it. Tony Sanchez and Bill Soliday looked surprised at first but then shrugged and joined in the chant.

"CUR-TIS! CUR-TIS!" The shout filled the room, and Curtis's look of horror turned to an ear-to-ear grin.

"ME-LIS-SA! ME-LIS-SA!" shouted Laura, Tammy, and Funny, sticking their chins in the air in defiance. Slowly other Riverfield kids began to join them.

"ME-LIS-SA! ME-LIS-SA!"

"CHRIS-TIE! CHRIS-TIE!" shouted Jana as Katie, Melanie, and Beth picked up the chant.

"CHRIS-TIE! CHRIS-TIE!"

Soon the room was filled with the mingled shouts of "CHRIS-TIE!" "ME-LIS-SA!" "CUR-TIS!" "CHRIS-TIE!" "ME-LIS-SA!" "CUR-TIS!"

CHAPTER

17

Jana, Katie, Beth, and Melanie were waiting at The Fabulous Five's special place by the school fence when Christie arrived.

"Well, today is the big day, Christie," said Melanie. "Whatever happens, I think we ran a *great* campaign."

"I still think Christie's going to win," said Beth. "She's really popular."

"She sure is," answered Katie. "The only thing that has me worried is Laura's promise to have a party for everyone who votes for Melissa if she wins."

"I agree," said Jana. "But I couldn't tell from all the shouting at Bumpers yesterday, when Whitney announced Curtis was the mystery candidate, which one of the candidates is the most popular. I just wonder who is *really* behind Curtis's campaign. I can't believe he and Whitney thought that up and did all those things by themselves. Besides, Curtis has too big an ego to keep a secret like that."

Christie took a deep breath and swallowed hard. "It was Jon and me."

Her friends went silent and turned to her with stunned looks on their faces. Their eyes were as big as saucers.

"*You?*" said Melanie in disbelief. The others stared at her with their mouths open.

"What do you mean, it was you?" asked Katie.

"Yeah? After all that work," said Beth.

Christie's heart almost burst at the feeling of having betrayed her friends.

"Wait a minute," said Jana softly. She looked deeply into Christie's eyes, and Christie gave her a silent plea for understanding. "Why did you do it, Christie?" Jana asked.

"I'm sorry, really I am. *But I just don't want to be class president.* I know you want me to be, and I appreciate your confidence in me. But if I were president, I'd have to give up things *I* really want to do, and I'm tired of doing that.

"My mother keeps pushing me to make good grades so I can be better than my brothers. My dad wants me to play competition tennis. The teachers all expect me to set an example for everyone else because I'm a principal's daughter. And now you want me to be class president and make all kinds of changes that you want. I love you all, but I don't want to do that." Christie's chin quivered and a tear ran down each cheek.

"Oh, my gosh," said Melanie.

"We didn't understand," said Katie, putting her hand on Christie's arm.

"Oh, we're so sorry," said Jana. "How could we have been such idiots?"

Her four friends gathered around Christie, locking her in a gigantic hug.

"You've got to forgive us," said Jana, holding Christie by the shoulders. "We got carried away and weren't thinking about you the way we should have."

Christie inhaled deeply and gave them a weak smile. "I know. And I didn't want to disappoint you, either. *Or* my parents. I had a talk with them this morning, too. At breakfast. I knew I had to prepare them in case I lose the election today."

"Gosh," said Jana. "That must have been hard."

"Not as hard as I thought it would be," Christie admitted. "They really do care about me, and they said they didn't realize that they were pushing me so hard. Dad even said he didn't mind if I played tennis just for fun from now on." She paused a minute. "I believe them. I just hope they remember not to push so hard the next time something comes up that they want me to do."

"You could still win," said Melanie.

"Sure," said Christie. "But you know, Curtis *is* a good candidate when you think about him. He is all the things Jon and I said on the posters and on the tape. I even think someday he may be a senator. Maybe even president."

Melanie and Beth looked at each other, covering their mouths and giggling at the thought.

"That was Jon's voice on the tape?" asked Jana.

"That's right," said Christie, laughing, too, at the thought of Jon's muffled voice and mysterious laugh.

"Okay!" said Jana, taking command. "This is what we're going to do. We've got to talk to as many Mark Twain kids as we can before we vote in homeroom. Tell everybody to vote for Curtis. Tell them THE FABU-LOUS FIVE said so." She held up high five, and the others hit it and cheered.

Christie worried all morning. Her friends had run around the school as fast as they could stopping every Mark Twain seventh-grader they saw and telling them to vote for Curtis. Randy Kirwan, Scott Daly, and Keith Masterson joined in to tell as many boys as they could. Jon and Whitney talked to the Copper Beach kids and told them that Christie wanted them to vote for Curtis. But would it be enough? She was still afraid she or Melissa might be elected when she marked her ballot during homeroom.

The cafeteria was noisier than usual when she went in for lunch. Her friends looked at her sympathetically when she sat down with them.

"Well, we did our best," said Katie.

Christie smiled at her and nodded. She was lucky to have four such great friends. If she had just not been so afraid of hurting them and had said what she was really thinking in the beginning, the five of them would have figured another way to beat Melissa and The Fantastic Foursome. She would know better next time. She would stick to the happy medium the way Jon had suggested and be more honest about her feelings. The thing that counted most was that The Fabulous Five were sticking together, as always.

"ATTENTION PLEASE," a voice came over the public address system. "FOLLOWING ARE THE RESULTS OF THE SCHOOL ELECTIONS."

Christie went tense as the names of the officers for the ninth and eighth grades were announced. Her hands went clammy as the announcements started for the seventh grade.

"TREASURER—RICHIE CORRIERRO."

A cheer went up around the table where Richie was sitting, and he stood up on the bench and waved his clenched hands in victory.

"SECRETARY—ELIZABETH HARVEY."

Everybody from Riverfield began yelling and clapping.

"VICE   PRESIDENT—MANDY   MCDER-MOTT."

A cheer went up from another part of the room for Mandy. "PRESIDENT—"

Christie had been holding her breath until she thought her lungs would burst.

"—CURTIS TROWBRIDGE."

She let out all the air she had been holding as Jana, Katie, Beth, and Melanie started pounding on her just as if she had won, and all five of them yelled for joy. She looked across the room and saw Jon with a big smile on his face. You know, she thought, I never knew losing could feel so good.

Two tables away she saw Laura turn to Melissa and frown. Uh-oh, thought Christie. The Fantastic Foursome may have lost the election, but they had to know that The Fabulous Five had thrown their support to Curtis. They wouldn't stand still for defeat by The Fabulous Five for very long. It was anyone's guess what they would try next.

Christie climbed into bed that night thinking that her day had been practically perfect. Curtis had won the election, and her friends and her parents all understood. And to top things off, Jon had taken her to meet his famous parents this evening. Wow, she thought. I'll be the envy of half the seventh grade.

Chip Smith and Marge Whitworth were really hyper. She had wondered if all television personalities were like that—acting as if they were on stage all the time. They were nice, but she could see how it would be difficult living with them.

After they had left his house, Jon had smiled at Christie and said, "Now that you've rescued my brain, how about tutoring me in tennis and helping me improve my backhand? It's pretty rotten."

"Sure," she had replied, returning his smile. "But I'll have to warn you that I may not be able to bring you all the way up from rotten to fabulous. You may have to settle for happy medium."

Now, snuggled under her covers, Christie thought about finding a happy medium. It made a lot of sense to her. She was herself instead of the person everyone had wanted her to be. Jon was himself, too, and not a cop-out. Everyone was happy—her friends, her parents, even Jon's parents. So, there was only one more thing that she absolutely had to do. Tomorrow she would begin concentrating on tennis and especially on improving Jon's *wonderfully* rotten backhand.

CHAPTER

18

*K*atie Shannon chewed on her pencil and watched Mona Vaughn and Matt Zeboski acting up in English Lit class. They were whispering and giggling together every time Miss Dickinson's back was turned. Didn't they know that they would get into trouble if she caught them? Katie thought with a frown. Maybe even get a detention?

She sighed and turned her attention back to her book and the story the class was supposed to be reading while their teacher wrote the homework assignment on the board. But she couldn't concentrate. This was Katie's big week. Her excitement had been growing and growing. Tomorrow they would announce the students who had been selected to be on the Teen Court, and her name just might be one of them. She could hardly stand the suspense.

Ever since she had found out that Mr. Bell, the principal, had decided to try a Teen Court instead of detentions as an experiment, she had wanted to be on it. Teen Court would be made up of three students from each class and two faculty members who would hear each complaint as if it were a court case. The court would establish the punishment for the ones found guilty. It would be an awesome responsibility, Katie thought, but it would give her a chance to express her feelings about a lot of things, such as the way girls were sometimes treated unfairly, and how some kids got away with things they shouldn't.

She smiled to herself. There were several seventh-graders running, but her record was excellent. She knew she had a super chance of being picked. She had never been in trouble in either elementary or at Wakeman Junior High. Not *one* detention. That had to count for a lot. And everyone knew that she was a no-nonsense person. Just the kind of person who should be on the Teen Court.

Katie relaxed in her seat. English Lit was one of her favorite subjects. She liked to read stories written by women authors such as Emily Brontë and Louisa May Alcott. It had made some of the boys in the class furious when Miss Dickinson announced that *Frankenstein* was written by Mary Shelley—*a woman*. She smiled to herself, remembering how they had booed.

The chattering and giggling in the next row was irritating her. She frowned at Mona Vaughn and Matt Zeboski again. They had been talking ever since they came into the classroom. So what if they had a big romance going? They should know better, and it wasn't fair to the rest of the class or Miss Dickinson.

Katie looked at the teacher. She still had her back turned. Teaching was hard enough without kids acting up, she thought. It miffed Katie when they did it.

She glanced again at Mona and Matt. This time she gave them an angry glare that she thought would stop them. Instead, they laughed at her, and Matt whispered something to Mona. Katie's face turned as red as her hair.

"You two had better stop!" she whispered angrily. "If Miss Dickinson catches you, you'll get a detention."

"Katie Shannon, come up to my desk!" Miss Dickinson's command hit Katie with the force of a Wakeman Warrior football player crashing into her. The teacher was standing by the desk with her hands on her hips, and she was looking directly at Katie.

Katie struggled out of her seat, and the room was deathly quiet as she walked to Miss Dickinson's desk. The aisle seemed a mile long, and she could feel everyone staring at her.

"Katie Shannon, I'm *amazed* at you, of all people. I didn't expect *you* to act up in class."

"But Miss Dickinson—"

"No arguments." She wrote hurriedly on a pink detention pad and then tore off the paper and gave it to Katie. "You deserve a detention when you cause a disturbance just the same as everyone else. Take this to Miss Wolfe after school today."

Katie was stunned. She had always been an exemplary student, and now she was being treated like Clarence Marshall and the other troublemakers in school. The piece of paper in her hand might as well have been a death sentence. Everyone would laugh at her now. But what was even worse, she might as well forget about being on the Teen Court.

What will happen to Katie's ambitions to be on Teen Court after she gets detention? Will she become the laughingstock of Wako Junior High, as she predicts? And how will she face her friends? Find out in *The Fabulous Five #4: Her Honor, Katie Shannon*.

ABOUT THE AUTHOR

Betsy Haynes, the daughter of a former news-
woman, began scribbling poetry and short stories as
soon as she learned to write. A serious writing career, however, had to wait until after her marriage
and the arrival of her two children. But that early
practice must have paid off, for within three months
Mrs. Haynes had sold her first story. In addition to a
number of magazine short stories and the Taffy Sinclair series, Mrs. Haynes is also the author of *The
Great Mom Swap* and its sequel, *The Great Boyfriend
Trap.* She lives in Colleyville, Texas, with her children and husband, who is also an author.

GOOD NEWS! The five best friends who formed the AGAINST TAFFY SINCLAIR CLUB will be starring in a series all their own.

IT'S NEW. IT'S FUN. IT'S FABULOUS. IT'S THE FABULOUS FIVE!

From Betsy Haynes, the bestselling author of the Taffy Sinclair books, *The Great Mom Swap*, and *The Great Boyfriend Trap*, comes THE FABULOUS FIVE. Follow the adventures of Jana Morgan and the rest of THE FABULOUS FIVE as they begin the new school year in Wakeman Jr. High.

☐ SEVENTH-GRADE RUMORS (Book #1)

The Fabulous Five are filled with anticipation, wondering how they'll fit into their new class at Wakeman Junior High. According to rumors, there's a group of girls called The Fantastic Foursome, whose leader is even prettier than Taffy Sinclair. Will the girls be able to overcome their rivalry to realize that rumors aren't always true? 15625-X $2.75

☐ THE TROUBLE WITH FLIRTING (Book #2)

Melanie Edwards insists that she *isn't* boy crazy. She just can't resist trying out some new flirting tips from a teen magazine on three different boys—her boyfriend from her old school, a boy from her new school, and a very cute eighth-grader! 15633-0 $2.75/$3.25 in Canada

☐ THE POPULARITY TRAP (Book #3)

When Christie Winchell is nominated for class president to run against perfect Melissa McConnell from The Fantastic Foursome, she feels pressure from all sides. Will the sudden appearance of a mystery candidate make her a winner after all? 15634-9 $2.75

HER HONOR, KATIE SHANNON (Book #4)

When Katie Shannon joins Wakeman High's new student court, she faces the difficult job of judging both her friends and foes. On Sale: December 15640-3 $2.75

Watch for a brand new book each and every month!

Book #5 On Sale: January/Book #6 On Sale: February

Buy them at your local bookstore or use this page to order:

Bantam Books, Dept. SK28, 414 East Golf Road, Des Plaines, IL 60016

Please send me the books I have checked above. I am enclosing $_____ (please add $2.00 to cover postage and handling). Send check or money order—no cash or C.O.D.s please.

Mr/Ms _____

Address _____

City/State _____ Zip _____

SK28—11/88

Please allow four to six weeks for delivery. This offer expires 5/89.

Skylark is Riding High with Books for Girls Who Love Horses!

☐ **A HORSE OF HER OWN by Joanna Campbell**
15564-4 $2.75
Like many 13-year-olds, Penny Rodgers has always longed to ride a horse. Since her parents won't pay for lessons, Penny decides to try her hand at training an old horse named Bones. When she turns him into a champion jumper, Penny proves to everyone that she's serious about riding!

☐ **RIDING HOME by Pamela Dryden**
15591-1 $2.50
Betsy Lawrence has loved horses all her life, and until her father's remarriage, was going to get her own horse! But now there's just not enough money. And Betsy can't help resenting her new stepsister Ferris, who is pretty, neat, does well in school, and gets all the music lessons she wants—Ferris loves music the way Betsy loves horses. Can the two girls ever learn to be sisters—and even friends?

New Series!

☐ **HORSE CRAZY: THE SADDLE CLUB: BOOK #1 by Bonnie Bryant**
15594-6 $2.95 Coming in September
Beginning with HORSE CRAZY: BOOK #1, this 10-book miniseries tells the stories of three very different girls with one thing in common: horses! Fun-loving Stevie and serious Carole are at Pine Hollow Stables for their usual lesson, when they meet another 12-year-old named Lisa. Her elaborate riding outfit prompts the girls to play a practical joke on her. After Lisa retaliates a truce is formed, and so is THE SADDLE CLUB! Look for HORSE SHY: BOOK #2, Coming in October!

Bantam Books, Dept. SK27, 414 East Golf Road, Des Plaines, IL 60016

Please send me the books I have checked above. I am enclosing $_____ (please add $2.00 to cover postage and handling). Send check or money order—no cash or C.O.D.s please.

Mr/Ms _____

Address _____

City/State _____ Zip _____

SK27—11/88

Please allow four to six weeks for delivery. This offer expires 5/89. Prices and availability subject to change without notice.

Great FREE offer
just for you!

Join SNEAK PEEKS™!

Do you want to know what's new before anyone else? Do you like to read great books about girls just like you? If you do, then you won't want to miss SNEAK PEEKS! Be the first of your friends to know what's hot ... When you join SNEAK PEEKS™, we'll send you FREE inside information in the mail about the latest books ... *before they're published!* Plus updates on your favorite series, authors, and exciting new stories filled with friendship and fun ... adventure and mystery ... girlfriends and boyfriends.

It's easy to be a member of SNEAK PEEKS™. Just fill out the coupon below ... and get ready for fun! It's FREE! Don't delay—sign up today!

Mail to: SNEAK PEEKS™,
Bantam Books, P.O. Box 1011,
South Holland, IL 60473

☐ YES! I want to be a member of Bantam's SNEAK PEEKS™ and receive hot-off-the-press information in the mail.

Name _____ Birthdate _____
Address _____
City/State _____ Zip _____
SK31—11/88